Tales of Troy: Ulysses the Sacker of Cities

Andrew Lang

Contents:

THE BOYHOOD AND PARENTS OF ULYSSES

Long ago, in a little island called Ithaca, on the west coast of Greece, there lived a king named Laertes. His kingdom was small and mountainous. People used to say that Ithaca "lay like a shield upon the sea, " which sounds as if it were a flat country. But in those times shields were very large, and rose at the middle into two peaks with a hollow between them, so that Ithaca, seen far off in the sea, with her two chief mountain peaks, and a cloven valley between them, looked exactly like a shield. The country was so rough that men kept no horses, for, at that time, people drove, standing up in little light chariots with two horses; they never rode, and there was no cavalry in battle: men fought from chariots. When Ulysses, the son of Laertes, King of Ithaca grew up, he never fought from a chariot, for he had none, but always on foot.

If there were no horses in Ithaca, there was plenty of cattle. The father of Ulysses had flocks of sheep, and herds of swine, and wild goats, deer, and hares lived in the hills and in the plains. The sea was full of fish of many sorts, which men caught with nets, and with rod and line and hook.

Thus Ithaca was a good island to live in. The summer was long, and there was hardly any winter; only a few cold weeks, and then the swallows came back, and the plains were like a garden, all covered with wild flowers—violets, lilies, narcissus, and roses. With the blue sky and the blue sea, the island was beautiful. White temples stood on the shores; and the Nymphs, a sort of fairies, had their little shrines built of stone, with wild rose-bushes hanging over them.

Other islands lay within sight, crowned with mountains, stretching away, one behind the other, into the sunset. Ulysses in the course of his life saw many rich countries, and great cities of men, but, wherever he was, his heart was always in the little isle of Ithaca, where he had learned how to row, and how to sail a boat, and how to shoot with bow and arrow, and to hunt boars and stags, and manage his hounds.

The mother of Ulysses was called Anticleia: she was the daughter of King Autolycus, who lived near Parnassus, a mountain on the mainland. This King Autolycus was the most cunning of men. He was a Master Thief, and could steal a man's pillow from under his head, but he does not seem to have been thought worse of for this. The Greeks had a God of Thieves, named Hermes, whom Autolycus worshipped, and people thought more good of his cunning tricks than harm of his dishonesty. Perhaps these tricks of his were only practised for amusement; however that may be, Ulysses became as artful as his grandfather; he was both the bravest and the most cunning of men, but Ulysses never stole things, except once, as we shall hear, from the enemy in time of war. He showed his cunning in stratagems of war, and in many strange escapes from giants and man-eaters.

Soon after Ulysses was born, his grandfather came to see his mother and father in Ithaca. He was sitting at supper when the nurse of Ulysses, whose name was Eurycleia, brought in the baby, and set him on the knees of Autolycus, saying, "Find a name for your grandson, for he is a child of many prayers. "

"I am very angry with many men and women in the world, " said Autolycus, "so let the child's name be *A Man of Wrath*, " which, in Greek, was Odysseus. So the child was called Odysseus by his own people, but the name was changed into Ulysses, and we shall call him Ulysses.

We do not know much about Ulysses when he was a little boy, except that he used to run about the garden with his father, asking questions, and begging that he might have fruit trees "for his very own. " He was a great pet, for his parents had no other son, so his father gave him thirteen pear trees, and forty fig trees, and promised him fifty rows of vines, all covered with grapes, which he could eat when he liked, without asking leave of the gardener. So he was not tempted to steal fruit, like his grandfather.

When Autolycus gave Ulysses his name, he said that he must come to stay with him, when he was a big boy, and he would get splendid presents. Ulysses was told about this, so, when he was a tall lad, he crossed the sea and drove in his chariot to the old man's house on Mount Parnassus. Everybody welcomed him, and next day his uncles and cousins and he went out to hunt a fierce wild boar, early in the morning. Probably Ulysses took his own dog, named Argos, the best of hounds, of which we shall hear again, long afterwards, for the dog lived to be very old. Soon the hounds came on the scent of a wild boar, and after them the men went, with spears in their hands, and Ulysses ran foremost, for he was already the swiftest runner in Greece.

He came on a great boar lying in a tangled thicket of boughs and bracken, a dark place where the sun never shone, nor could the rain pierce through. Then the noise of the men's shouts and the barking of the dogs awakened the boar, and up he sprang, bristling all over his back, and with fire shining from his eyes. In rushed Ulysses first of all, with his spear raised to strike, but the boar was too quick for him, and ran in, and drove his sharp tusk sideways, ripping up the thigh of Ulysses. But the boar's tusk missed the bone, and Ulysses sent his sharp spear into the beast's right shoulder, and the spear went clean through, and the boar fell dead, with a loud cry. The uncles of Ulysses bound up his wound carefully, and sang a magical song over it, as the French soldiers wanted to do to Joan of Arc when the arrow pierced her shoulder at the siege of Orleans. Then the blood ceased to flow, and soon Ulysses was quite healed of his wound. They thought that he would be a good warrior, and gave him splendid presents, and when he went home again he told all that had happened to his father and mother, and his nurse, Eurycleia. But there was always a long white mark or scar above his left knee, and about that scar we shall hear again, many years afterwards.

HOW PEOPLE LIVED IN THE TIME OF ULYSSES

When Ulysses was a young man he wished to marry a princess of his own rank. Now there were at that time many kings in Greece, and you must be told how they lived. Each king had his own little kingdom, with his chief town, walled with huge walls of enormous stone. Many of these walls are still standing, though the grass has grown over the ruins of most of them, and in later years, men believed that those walls must have been built by giants, the stones are so enormous. Each king had nobles under him, rich men, and all had their palaces, each with its courtyard, and its long hall, where the fire burned in the midst, and the King and Queen sat beside it on high thrones, between the four chief carved pillars that held up the roof. The thrones were made of cedar wood and ivory, inlaid with gold, and there were many other chairs and small tables for guests, and the walls and doors were covered with bronze plates, and gold and silver, and sheets of blue glass. Sometimes they were painted with pictures of bull hunts, and a few of these pictures may still be seen. At night torches were lit, and placed in the hands of golden figures of boys, but all the smoke of fire and torches escaped by a hole in the roof, and made the ceiling black. On the walls hung swords and spears and helmets and shields, which needed to be often cleaned from the stains of the smoke. The minstrel or poet sat beside the King and Queen, and, after supper he struck his harp, and sang stories of old wars. At night the King and Queen slept in their own place, and the women in their own rooms; the princesses had their chambers upstairs, and the young princes had each his room built separate in the courtyard.

There were bath rooms with polished baths, where guests were taken when they arrived dirty from a journey. The guests lay at night on beds in the portico, for the climate was warm. There were plenty of servants, who were usually slaves taken in war, but they were very kindly treated, and were friendly with their masters. No coined money was used; people paid for things in cattle, or in weighed pieces of gold. Rich men had plenty of gold cups, and gold-hilted swords, and bracelets, and brooches. The kings were the leaders in war and judges in peace, and did sacrifices to the Gods, killing cattle and swine and sheep, on which they afterwards dined.

They dressed in a simple way, in a long smock of linen or silk, which fell almost to the feet, but was tucked up into a belt round the waist, and worn longer or shorter, as they happened to choose. Where it needed fastening at the throat, golden brooches were used, beautifully made, with safety pins. This garment was much like the plaid that the Highlanders used to wear, with its belt and brooches. Over it the Greeks wore great cloaks of woollen cloth when the weather was cold, but these they did not use in battle. They fastened their breastplates, in war, over their smocks, and had other armour covering the lower parts of the body, and leg armour called "greaves"; while the great shield which guarded the whole body from throat to ankles was carried by a broad belt slung round the neck. The sword was worn in another belt, crossing the shield belt. They had light shoes in peace, and higher and heavier boots in war, or for walking across country.

The women wore the smock, with more brooches and jewels than the men; and had head coverings, with veils, and mantles over all, and necklaces of gold and amber, earrings, and bracelets of gold or of bronze. The colours of their dresses were various, chiefly white and purple; and, when in mourning, they wore very dark blue, not black. All the armour, and the sword blades and spearheads were made, not of steel or iron, but of bronze, a mixture of copper and tin. The shields were made of several thicknesses of leather, with a plating of bronze above; tools, such as axes and ploughshares, were either of iron or bronze; and so were the blades of knives and daggers.

To us the houses and way of living would have seemed very splendid, and also, in some ways, rather rough. The palace floors, at least in the house of Ulysses, were littered with bones and feet of the oxen slain for food, but this happened when Ulysses had been long from home. The floor of the hall in the house of Ulysses was not boarded with planks, or paved with stone: it was made of clay; for he was a poor king of small islands. The cooking was coarse: a pig or sheep was killed, roasted and eaten immediately. We never hear of boiling meat, and though people probably ate fish, we do not hear of their doing so, except when no meat could be procured. Still some people must have liked them; for in the pictures that were painted or cut in precious stones in these times we see the half-naked fisherman walking home, carrying large fish.

The people were wonderful workers of gold and bronze. Hundreds of their golden jewels have been found in their graves, but probably these were made and buried two or three centuries before the time of Ulysses. The dagger blades had pictures of fights with lions, and of

5

flowers, inlaid on them, in gold of various colours, and in silver; nothing so beautiful is made now. There are figures of men hunting bulls on some of the gold cups, and these are wonderfully life-like. The vases and pots of earthenware were painted in charming patterns: in short, it was a splendid world to live in.

The people believed in many Gods, male and female, under the chief God, Zeus. The Gods were thought to be taller than men, and immortal, and to live in much the same way as men did, eating, drinking, and sleeping in glorious palaces. Though they were supposed to reward good men, and to punish people who broke their oaths and were unkind to strangers, there were many stories told in which the Gods were fickle, cruel, selfish, and set very bad examples to men. How far these stories were believed is not sure; it is certain that "all men felt a need of the Gods, " and thought that they were pleased by good actions and displeased by evil. Yet, when a man felt that his behaviour had been bad, he often threw the blame on the Gods, and said that they had misled him, which really meant no more than that "he could not help it. "

There was a curious custom by which the princes bought wives from the fathers of the princesses, giving cattle and gold, and bronze and iron, but sometimes a prince got a wife as the reward for some very brave action. A man would not give his daughter to a wooer whom she did not love, even if he offered the highest price, at least this must have been the general rule, for husbands and wives were very fond of each other, and of their children, and husbands always allowed their wives to rule the house, and give their advice on everything. It was thought a very wicked thing for a woman to like another man better than her husband, and there were few such wives, but among them was the most beautiful woman who ever lived.

THE WOOING OF HELEN OF THE FAIR HANDS

This was the way in which people lived when Ulysses was young, and wished to be married. The worst thing in the way of life was that the greatest and most beautiful princesses might be taken prisoners, and carried off as slaves to the towns of the men who had killed their fathers and husbands. Now at that time one lady was far the fairest in the world: namely, Helen, daughter of King Tyndarus. Every young prince heard of her and desired to marry her; so her father invited them all to his palace, and entertained them, and found out what they would give. Among the rest Ulysses went, but his father had a little kingdom, a rough island, with others near it, and Ulysses had not a good chance. He was not tall; though very strong and active, he was a short man with broad shoulders, but his face was handsome, and, like all the princes, he wore long yellow hair, clustering like a hyacinth flower. His manner was rather hesitating, and he seemed to speak very slowly at first, though afterwards his words came freely. He was good at everything a man can do; he could plough, and build houses, and make ships, and he was the best archer in Greece, except one, and could bend the great bow of a dead king, Eurytus, which no other man could string. But he had no horses, and had no great train of followers; and, in short, neither Helen nor her father thought of choosing Ulysses for her husband out of so many tall, handsome young princes, glittering with gold ornaments. Still, Helen was very kind to Ulysses, and there was great friendship between them, which was fortunate for her in the end.

Tyndarus first made all the princes take an oath that they would stand by the prince whom he chose, and would fight for him in all his quarrels. Then he named for her husband Menelaus, King of Lacedaemon. He was a very brave man, but not one of the strongest; he was not such a fighter as the gigantic Aias, the tallest and strongest of men; or as Diomede, the friend of Ulysses; or as his own brother, Agamemnon, the King of the rich city of Mycenae, who was chief over all other princes, and general of the whole army in war. The great lions carved in stone that seemed to guard his city are still standing above the gate through which Agamemnon used to drive his chariot.

The man who proved to be the best fighter of all, Achilles, was not among the lovers of Helen, for he was still a boy, and his mother, Thetis of the silver feet, a goddess of the sea, had sent him to be brought up as a girl, among the daughters of Lycomedes of Scyros, in an island far away. Thetis did this because Achilles was her only child, and there was a prophecy that, if he went to the wars, he would win the greatest glory, but die very young, and never see his mother again. She thought that if war broke out he would not be found hiding in girl's dress, among girls, far away.

So at last, after thinking over the matter for long, Tyndarus gave fair Helen to Menelaus, the rich King of Lacedaemon; and her twin sister Clytaemnestra, who was also very beautiful, was given to King Agamemnon, the chief over all the princes. They all lived very happily together at first, but not for long.

In the meantime King Tyndarus spoke to his brother Icarius, who had a daughter named Penelope. She also was very pretty, but not nearly so beautiful as her cousin, fair Helen, and we know that Penelope was not very fond of her cousin. Icarius, admiring the strength and wisdom of Ulysses, gave him his daughter Penelope to be his wife, and Ulysses loved her very dearly, no man and wife were ever dearer to each other. They went away together to rocky Ithaca, and perhaps Penelope was not sorry that a wide sea lay between her home and that of Helen; for Helen was not only the fairest woman that ever lived in the world, but she was so kind and gracious and charming that no man could see her without loving her. When she was only a child, the famous prince Theseus, who was famous in Greek Story, carried her away to his own city of Athens, meaning to marry her when she grew up, and even at that time, there was a war for her sake, for her brothers followed Theseus with an army, and fought him, and brought her home.

She had fairy gifts; for instance, she had a great red jewel, called "the Star, " and when she wore it red drops seemed to fall from it and vanished before they touched and stained her white breast—so white that people called her "the Daughter of the Swan. " She could speak in the very voice of any man or woman, so folk also named her Echo, and it was believed that she could neither grow old nor die, but would at last pass away to the Elysian plain and the world's end, where life is easiest for men. No snow comes thither, nor great storm, nor any rain; but always the river of Ocean that rings round the whole earth sends forth the west wind to blow cool on the people of King Rhadamanthus of the fair hair. These were some of the stories that men told of fair Helen, but Ulysses was never sorry that he had not the fortune to marry her, so fond he was of her cousin, his wife, Penelope, who was very wise and good.

When Ulysses brought his wife home they lived, as the custom was, in the palace of his father, King Laertes, but Ulysses, with his own hands, built a chamber for Penelope and himself. There grew a great olive tree in the inner court of the palace, and its stem was as large as one of the tall carved pillars of the hall. Round about this tree Ulysses built the chamber, and finished it with close-set stones, and roofed it over, and made close-fastening doors. Then he cut off all the branches of the olive tree, and smoothed the trunk, and shaped it into the bed-post, and made the bedstead beautiful with inlaid work of gold and silver and ivory. There was no such bed in Greece, and no man could move it from its place, and this bed comes again into the story, at the very end.

Now time went by, and Ulysses and Penelope had one son called Telemachus; and Eurycleia, who had been his father's nurse, took care of him. They were all very happy, and lived in peace in rocky Ithaca, and Ulysses looked after his lands, and flocks, and herds, and went hunting with his dog Argos, the swiftest of hounds.

THE STEALING OF HELEN

This happy time did not last long, and Telemachus was still a baby, when war arose, so great and mighty and marvellous as had never been known in the world. Far across the sea that lies on the east of Greece, there dwelt the rich King Priam. His town was called Troy, or Ilios, and it stood on a hill near the seashore, where are the straits of Hellespont, between Europe and Asia; it was a great city surrounded by strong walls, and its ruins are still standing. The kings could make merchants who passed through the straits pay toll to them, and they had allies in Thrace, a part of Europe opposite Troy, and Priam was chief of all princes on his side of the sea, as Agamemnon was chief king in Greece. Priam had many beautiful things; he had a vine made of gold, with golden leaves and clusters, and he had the swiftest horses, and many strong and brave sons; the strongest and bravest was named Hector, and the youngest and most beautiful was named Paris.

There was a prophecy that Priam's wife would give birth to a burning torch, so, when Paris was born, Priam sent a servant to carry the baby into a wild wood on Mount Ida, and leave him to die or be eaten by wolves and wild cats. The servant left the child, but a shepherd found him, and brought him up as his own son. The boy became as beautiful, for a boy, as Helen was for a girl, and was the best runner, and hunter, and archer among the country people. He was loved by the beautiful OEnone, a nymph—that is, a kind of fairy—who dwelt in a cave among the woods of Ida. The Greeks and Trojans believed in these days that such fair nymphs haunted all beautiful woodland places, and the mountains, and wells, and had crystal palaces, like mermaids, beneath the waves of the sea. These fairies were not mischievous, but gentle and kind. Sometimes they married mortal men, and OEnone was the bride of Paris, and hoped to keep him for her own all the days of his life.

It was believed that she had the magical power of healing wounded men, however sorely they were hurt. Paris and OEnone lived most happily together in the forest; but one day, when the servants of Priam had driven off a beautiful bull that was in the herd of Paris, he left the hills to seek it, and came into the town of Troy. His mother, Hecuba, saw him, and looking at him closely, perceived that he wore a ring which she had tied round her baby's neck when he was taken away from her soon after his birth. Then Hecuba, beholding him so beautiful, and knowing him to be her son, wept for joy, and they all forgot the prophecy that he would be a burning torch of fire, and Priam gave him a house like those of his brothers, the Trojan princes.

The fame of beautiful Helen reached Troy, and Paris quite forgot unhappy OEnone, and must needs go to see Helen for himself. Perhaps he meant to try to win her for his wife, before her marriage. But sailing was little understood in these times, and the water was wide, and men were often driven for years out of their course, to Egypt, and Africa, and far away into the unknown seas, where fairies lived in enchanted islands, and cannibals dwelt in caves of the hills.

Paris came much too late to have a chance of marrying Helen; however, he was determined to see her, and he made his way to her palace beneath the mountain Taygetus, beside the clear swift river Eurotas. The servants came out of the hall when they heard the sound of wheels and horses' feet, and some of them took the horses to the stables, and tilted the chariots against the gateway, while others led Paris into the hall, which shone like the sun with gold and silver. Then Paris and his companions were led to the baths, where they were bathed, and clad in new clothes, mantles of white, and robes of purple, and next they were brought before King Menelaus, and he welcomed them kindly, and meat was set before them, and wine in cups of gold. While they were talking, Helen came forth from her fragrant chamber, like a Goddess, her maidens following her, and carrying for her an ivory distaff with violet-coloured wool, which she span as she sat, and heard Paris tell how far he had travelled to see her who was so famous for her beauty even in countries far away.

Then Paris knew that he had never seen, and never could see, a lady so lovely and gracious as Helen as she sat and span, while the red drops fell and vanished from the ruby called the Star; and Helen knew that among all the princes in the world there was none so beautiful as Paris. Now some say that Paris, by art magic, put on the appearance of Menelaus, and asked Helen to come sailing with him, and that she, thinking he was her husband, followed him, and he carried her across the wide waters of Troy, away from her lord and her one beautiful little daughter, the child Hermione. And others say that the Gods carried Helen herself off to Egypt, and that they made in her likeness a beautiful ghost, out of flowers and sunset clouds, whom Paris bore to Troy, and this they did to cause war between

Greeks and Trojans. Another story is that Helen and her bower maiden and her jewels were seized by force, when Menelaus was out hunting. It is only certain that Paris and Helen did cross the seas together, and that Menelaus and little Hermione were left alone in the melancholy palace beside the Eurotas. Penelope, we know for certain, made no excuses for her beautiful cousin, but hated her as the cause of her own sorrows and of the deaths of thousands of men in war, for all the Greek princes were bound by their oath to fight for Menelaus against any one who injured him and stole his wife away. But Helen was very unhappy in Troy, and blamed herself as bitterly as all the other women blamed her, and most of all OEnone, who had been the love of Paris. The men were much more kind to Helen, and were determined to fight to the death rather than lose the sight of her beauty among them.

The news of the dishonour done to Menelaus and to all the princes of Greece ran through the country like fire through a forest. East and west and south and north went the news: to kings in their castles on the hills, and beside the rivers and on cliffs above the sea. The cry came to ancient Nestor of the white beard at Pylos, Nestor who had reigned over two generations of men, who had fought against the wild folk of the hills, and remembered the strong Heracles, and Eurytus of the black bow that sang before the day of battle.

The cry came to black-bearded Agamemnon, in his strong town called "golden Mycenae, " because it was so rich; it came to the people in Thisbe, where the wild doves haunt; and it came to rocky Pytho, where is the sacred temple of Apollo and the maid who prophesies. It came to Aias, the tallest and strongest of men, in his little isle of Salamis; and to Diomede of the loud war-cry, the bravest of warriors, who held Argos and Tiryns of the black walls of huge, stones, that are still standing. The summons came to the western islands and to Ulysses in Ithaca, and even far south to the great island of Crete of the hundred cities, where Idomeneus ruled in Cnossos; Idomeneus, whose ruined palace may still be seen with the throne of the king, and pictures painted on the walls, and the King's own draught-board of gold and silver, and hundreds of tablets of clay, on which are written the lists of royal treasures. Far north went the news to Pelasgian Argos, and Hellas, where the people of Peleus dwelt, the Myrmidons; but Peleus was too old to fight, and his boy, Achilles, dwelt far away, in the island of Scyros, dressed as a girl, among the daughters of King Lycomedes. To many another town and to a hundred islands went the bitter news of approaching war, for all princes knew that their honour and their oaths compelled them to gather their spearmen, and bowmen, and slingers from the fields and the fishing, and to make ready their ships, and meet King Agamemnon in the harbour of Aulis, and cross the wide sea to besiege Troy town.

Now the story is told that Ulysses was very unwilling to leave his island and his wife Penelope, and little Telemachus; while Penelope had no wish that he should pass into danger, and into the sight of Helen of the fair hands. So it is said that when two of the princes came to summon Ulysses, he pretended to be mad, and went ploughing the sea sand with oxen, and sowing the sand with salt. Then the prince Palamedes took the baby Telemachus from the arms of his nurse, Eurycleia, and laid him in the line of the furrow, where the ploughshare would strike him and kill him. But Ulysses turned the plough aside, and they cried that he was not mad, but sane, and he must keep his oath, and join the fleet at Aulis, a long voyage for him to sail, round the stormy southern Cape of Maleia.

Whether this tale be true or not, Ulysses did go, leading twelve black ships, with high beaks painted red at prow and stern. The ships had oars, and the warriors manned the oars, to row when there was no wind. There was a small raised deck at each end of the ships; on these decks men stood to fight with sword and spear when there was a battle at sea. Each ship had but one mast, with a broad lugger sail, and for anchors they had only heavy stones attached to cables. They generally landed at night, and slept on the shore of one of the many islands, when they could, for they greatly feared to sail out of sight of land.

The fleet consisted of more than a thousand ships, each with fifty warriors, so the army was of more than fifty thousand men. Agamemnon had a hundred ships, Diomede had eighty, Nestor had ninety, the Cretans with Idomeneus, had eighty, Menelaus had sixty; but Aias and Ulysses, who lived in small islands, had only twelve ships apiece. Yet Aias was so brave and strong, and Ulysses so brave and wise, that they were ranked among the greatest chiefs and advisers of Agamemnon, with Menelaus, Diomede, Idomeneus, Nestor, Menestheus of Athens, and two or three others. These chiefs were called the Council, and gave advice to Agamemnon, who was commander-in-chief. He was a brave fighter, but so anxious and fearful of losing the lives of his soldiers that Ulysses and Diomede were often obliged to speak to him very severely. Agamemnon was also very insolent and greedy, though, when anybody stood up to him, he was ready to apologise, for fear the injured chief should renounce his service and take away his soldiers.

Nestor was much respected because he remained brave, though he was too old to be very useful in battle. He generally tried to make peace when the princes quarrelled with Agamemnon. He loved to tell long stories about his great deeds when he was young, and he wished the chiefs to fight in old-fashioned ways.

For instance, in his time the Greeks had fought in clan regiments, and the princely men had never dismounted in battle, but had fought in squadrons of chariots, but now the owners of chariots fought on foot, each man for himself, while his squire kept the chariot near him to escape on if he had to retreat. Nestor wished to go back to the good old way of chariot charges against the crowds of foot soldiers of the enemy. In short, he was a fine example of the old-fashioned soldier.

Aias, though so very tall, strong, and brave, was rather stupid. He seldom spoke, but he was always ready to fight, and the last to retreat. Menelaus was weak of body, but as brave as the best, or more brave, for he had a keen sense of honour, and would attempt what he had not the strength to do. Diomede and Ulysses were great friends, and always fought side by side, when they could, and helped each other in the most dangerous adventures.

These were the chiefs who led the great Greek armada from the harbour of Aulis. A long time had passed, after the flight of Helen, before the large fleet could be collected, and more time went by in the attempt to cross the sea to Troy. There were tempests that scattered the ships, so they were driven back to Aulis to refit; and they fought, as they went out again, with the peoples of unfriendly islands, and besieged their towns. What they wanted most of all was to have Achilles with them, for he was the leader of fifty ships and 2,500 men, and he had magical armour made, men said, for his father, by Hephaestus, the God of armour-making and smithy work.

At last the fleet came to the Isle of Scyros, where they suspected that Achilles was concealed. King Lycomedes received the chiefs kindly, and they saw all his beautiful daughters dancing and playing at ball, but Achilles was still so young and slim and so beautiful that they did not know him among the others. There was a prophecy that they could not take Troy without him, and yet they could not find him out. Then Ulysses had a plan. He blackened his eyebrows and beard and put on the dress of a Phoenician merchant. The Phoenicians were a people who lived near the Jews, and were of the same race, and spoke much the same language, but, unlike the Jews, who, at that time were farmers in Palestine, tilling the ground, and keeping flocks and herds, the Phoenicians were the greatest of traders and sailors, and stealers of slaves. They carried cargoes of beautiful cloths, and embroideries, and jewels of gold, and necklaces of amber, and sold these everywhere about the shores of Greece and the islands.

Ulysses then dressed himself like a Phoenician pedlar, with his pack on his back: he only took a stick in his hand, his long hair was turned up, and hidden under a red sailor's cap, and in this figure he came, stooping beneath his pack, into the courtyard of King Lycomedes. The girls heard that a pedlar had come, and out they all ran, Achilles with the rest to watch the pedlar undo his pack. Each chose what she liked best: one took a wreath of gold; another a necklace of gold and amber; another earrings; a fourth a set of brooches, another a dress of embroidered scarlet cloth; another a veil; another a pair of bracelets; but at the bottom of the pack lay a great sword of bronze, the hilt studded with golden nails. Achilles seized the sword. "This is for me! " he said, and drew the sword from the gilded sheath, and made it whistle round his head.

"You are Achilles, Peleus' son! " said Ulysses; "and you are to be the chief warrior of the Achaeans, " for the Greeks then called themselves Achaeans. Achilles was only too glad to hear these words, for he was quite tired of living among maidens. Ulysses led him into the hall where the chiefs were sitting at their wine, and Achilles was blushing like any girl.

"Here is the Queen of the Amazons, " said Ulysses—for the Amazons were a race of warlike maidens—"or rather here is Achilles, Peleus' son, with sword in hand. " Then they all took his hand, and welcomed him, and he was clothed in man's dress, with the sword by his side, and presently they sent him back with ten ships to his home. There his mother, Thetis, of the silver feet, the goddess of the sea, wept over him, saying, "My child, thou hast the choice of a long and happy and peaceful life here with me, or of a brief time of war and undying renown. Never shall I see thee again in Argos if thy choice is for war. " But Achilles chose to die young, and to be famous as long as the world stands. So his father gave him fifty ships, with Patroclus, who was older than he, to be his friend, and with an old man, Phoenix, to advise him; and his mother gave him the glorious armour that the God had made for his father, and the heavy ashen spear that none but he could wield, and he sailed to join the host of the Achaeans, who all praised and thanked Ulysses that had found for them such a prince. For Achilles was the fiercest fighter of them all, and the swiftest-footed man, and the most courteous prince, and the gentlest with women and children, but he was proud and high of heart, and when he was angered his anger was terrible.

The Trojans would have had no chance against the Greeks if only the men of the city of Troy had fought to keep Helen of the fair hands. But they had allies, who spoke different languages, and came to fight for them both from Europe and from Asia. On the Trojan as well as on the Greek side were people called Pelasgians, who seem to have lived on both shores of the sea. There were Thracians, too, who dwelt much further north than Achilles, in Europe and beside the strait of Hellespont, where the narrow sea runs like a river. There were warriors of Lycia, led by Sarpedon and Glaucus; there were Carians, who spoke in a strange tongue; there were Mysians and men from Alybe, which was called "the birthplace of silver, " and many other peoples sent their armies, so that the war was between Eastern Europe, on one side, and Western Asia Minor on the other. The people of Egypt took no part in the war: the Greeks and Islesmen used to come down in their ships and attack the Egyptians as the Danes used to invade England. You may see the warriors from the islands, with their horned helmets, in old Egyptian pictures.

The commander-in-chief, as we say now, of the Trojans was Hector, the son of Priam. He was thought a match for any one of the Greeks, and was brave and good. His brothers also were leaders, but Paris preferred to fight from a distance with bow and arrows. He and Pandarus, who dwelt on the slopes of Mount Ida, were the best archers in the Trojan army. The princes usually fought with heavy spears, which they threw at each other, and with swords, leaving archery to the common soldiers who had no armour of bronze. But Teucer, Meriones, and Ulysses were the best archers of the Achaeans. People called Dardanians were led by Aeneas, who was said to be the son of the most beautiful of the goddesses. These, with Sarpedon and Glaucus, were the most famous of the men who fought for Troy.

Troy was a strong town on a hill. Mount Ida lay behind it, and in front was a plain sloping to the sea shore. Through this plain ran two beautiful clear rivers, and there were scattered here and there what you would have taken for steep knolls, but they were really mounds piled up over the ashes of warriors who had died long ago. On these mounds sentinels used to stand and look across the water to give warning if the Greek fleet drew near, for the Trojans had heard that it was on its way. At last the fleet came in view, and the sea was black with ships, the oarsmen pulling with all their might for the honour of being the first to land. The race was won by the ship of the prince Protesilaus, who was first of all to leap on shore, but as he leaped he was struck to the heart by an arrow from the bow of Paris. This must have seemed a good omen to the Trojans, and to the Greeks evil, but we do not hear that the landing was resisted in great force, any more than that of Norman William was, when he invaded England.

The Greeks drew up all their ships on shore, and the men camped in huts built in front of the ships. There was thus a long row of huts with the ships behind them, and in these huts the Greeks lived all through the ten years that the siege of Troy lasted. In these days they do not seem to have understood how to conduct a siege. You would have expected the Greeks to build towers and dig trenches all round Troy, and from the towers watch the roads, so that provisions might not be brought in from the country. This is called "investing" a town, but the Greeks never invested Troy. Perhaps they had not men enough; at all events the place remained open, and cattle could always be driven in to feed the warriors and the women and children.

Moreover, the Greeks for long never seem to have tried to break down one of the gates, nor to scale the walls, which were very high, with ladders. On the other hand, the Trojans and allies never ventured to drive the Greeks into the sea; they commonly remained within the walls or skirmished just beneath them. The older men insisted on this way of fighting, in spite of Hector, who always wished to attack and storm the camp of the Greeks. Neither side had machines for throwing heavy stones, such as the Romans used later, and the most that the Greeks did was to follow Achilles and capture small neighbouring cities, and take the women for slaves, and drive the cattle. They got provisions and wine from the Phoenicians, who came in ships, and made much profit out of the war.

It was not till the tenth year that the war began in real earnest, and scarcely any of the chief leaders had fallen. Fever came upon the Greeks, and all day the camp was black with smoke, and all night shone with fire from the great piles of burning wood, on which the Greeks burned their dead, whose bones they then buried under hillocks of earth. Many of these hillocks are still standing on the plain of Troy. When the plague had raged for ten days, Achilles called an assembly of the whole army, to try to find out why the Gods were angry. They thought that the beautiful God Apollo (who took the Trojan side) was shooting invisible arrows at them from his silver bow, though fevers in armies are usually caused by dirt and drinking bad water. The great heat of the sun, too, may have helped to cause the disease; but we must tell the story as the Greeks told it themselves. So Achilles spoke in the assembly, and proposed to ask some prophet why Apollo was angry. The chief prophet was Calchas. He rose and said that he would declare the truth if Achilles would promise to protect him from the anger of any prince whom the truth might offend.

Achilles knew well whom Calchas meant. Ten days before, a priest of Apollo had come to the camp and offered ransom for his daughter Chryseis, a beautiful girl, whom Achilles had taken prisoner, with many others, when he captured a small town. Chryseis had been given as a slave to Agamemnon, who always got the best of the plunder because he was chief king, whether he had taken part in the fighting or not. As a rule he did not. To Achilles had been given another girl, Briseis, of whom he was very fond. Now when Achilles had promised to protect Calchas, the prophet spoke out, and boldly said, what all men knew already, that Apollo caused the plague because Agamemnon would not return Chryseis, and had insulted her father, the priest of the God.

On hearing this, Agamemnon was very angry. He said that he would send Chryseis home, but that he would take Briseis away from Achilles. Then Achilles was drawing his great sword from the sheath to kill Agamemnon, but even in his anger he knew that this was wrong, so he merely called Agamemnon a greedy coward, "with face of dog and heart of deer, " and he swore that he and his men would fight no more against the Trojans. Old Nestor tried to make peace, and swords were not drawn, but Briseis was taken away from Achilles, and Ulysses put Chryseis on board of his ship and sailed away with her to her father's town, and gave her up to her father. Then her father prayed to Apollo that the plague might cease, and it did cease—when the Greeks had cleansed their camp, and purified themselves and cast their filth into the sea.

We know how fierce and brave Achilles was, and we may wonder that he did not challenge Agamemnon to fight a duel. But the Greeks never fought duels, and Agamemnon was believed to be chief king by right divine. Achilles went alone to the sea shore when his dear Briseis was led away, and he wept, and called to his mother, the silver-footed lady of the waters. Then she arose from the grey sea, like a mist, and sat down beside her son, and stroked his hair with her hand, and he told her all his sorrows. So she said that she would go up to the dwelling of the Gods, and pray Zeus, the chief of them all, to make the Trojans win a great battle, so that Agamemnon should feel his need of Achilles, and make amends for his insolence, and do him honour.

Thetis kept her promise, and Zeus gave his word that the Trojans should defeat the Greeks. That night Zeus sent a deceitful dream to Agamemnon. The dream took the shape of old Nestor, and said that Zeus would give him victory that day. While he was still asleep, Agamemnon was fun of hope that he would instantly take Troy, but, when he woke, he seems not to have been nearly so confident, for in place of putting on his armour, and bidding the Greeks arm themselves, he merely dressed in his robe and mantle, took his sceptre, and went and told the chiefs about his dream. They did not feel much encouraged, so he said that he would try the temper of the army. He would call them together, and propose to return to Greece; but, if the soldiers took him at his word, the other chiefs were to stop them. This was a foolish plan, for the soldiers were wearying for beautiful Greece, and their homes, and wives and children. Therefore, when Agamemnon did as he had said, the whole army rose, like the sea under the west wind, and, with a shout, they rushed to the ships, while the dust blew in clouds from under their feet. Then they began to launch their ships, and it seems that the princes were carried away in the rush, and were as eager as the rest to go home.

But Ulysses only stood in sorrow and anger beside his ship, and never put hand to it, for he felt how disgraceful it was to run away. At last he threw down his mantle, which his herald Eurybates of Ithaca, a round-shouldered, brown, curly-haired man, picked up, and he ran to find Agamemnon, and took his sceptre, a gold-studded staff, like a marshal's baton, and he gently told the chiefs whom he met that they were doing a shameful thing; but he drove the common soldiers back to the place of meeting with the sceptre. They all returned, puzzled and chattering, but one lame, bandy-legged, bald, round-shouldered, impudent fellow, named Thersites, jumped up and made an insolent speech, insulting the princes, and advising the army to run away. Then Ulysses took him and beat him till the blood came, and he sat down, wiping away his tears, and looking so foolish that the whole army laughed at him, and cheered Ulysses when he and Nestor bade them arm and fight. Agamemnon still believed a good deal in his dream, and prayed that he might take Troy that very day, and kill Hector. Thus Ulysses alone saved the army from a cowardly retreat; but for him the ships would have been launched in an hour. But the Greeks armed and advanced in full force, all except Achilles and his friend Patroclus with their two or three thousand men. The Trojans also took heart, knowing that Achilles would not fight, and the armies approached each other. Paris himself, with two spears and a bow, and without armour, walked into the space between the hosts, and challenged any Greek prince to single combat. Menelaus, whose wife Paris had carried away, was as glad as a hungry lion when he finds a stag or a goat, and leaped in armour from his chariot, but Paris turned and slunk away, like a man when he meets a great serpent on a narrow path in the hills. Then Hector rebuked Paris for his cowardice, and Paris was ashamed and offered to end the war by fighting Menelaus. If he himself fell, the Trojans must give up Helen and all her jewels; if Menelaus fell, the Greeks were to return without fair Helen. The Greeks accepted this plan, and both sides disarmed themselves to look on at the fight in comfort, and they meant to take the most solemn oaths to keep peace till the combat was lost and won, and the quarrel settled. Hector sent into Troy for two lambs, which were to be sacrificed when the oaths were taken.

In the meantime Helen of the fair hands was at home working at a great purple tapestry on which she embroidered the battles of the Greeks and Trojans. It was just like the tapestry at Bayeux on which Norman ladies embroidered the battles in the Norman Conquest of England. Helen was very fond of embroidering, like poor Mary, Queen of Scots, when a prisoner in Loch Leven Castle. Probably the work kept both Helen and Mary from thinking of their past lives and their sorrows.

When Helen heard that her husband was to fight Paris, she wept, and threw a shining veil over her head, and with her two bower maidens went to the roof of the gate tower, where king Priam was sitting with the old Trojan chiefs. They saw her and said that it was small blame to fight for so beautiful a lady, and Priam called her "dear child, " and said, "I do not blame you, I blame the Gods who brought about this war. " But Helen said that she wished she had died before she left her little daughter and her husband, and her home: "Alas! shameless me! " Then she told Priam the names of the chief Greek warriors, and of Ulysses, who was shorter by a head than Agamemnon, but broader in chest and shoulders. She wondered that she could not see her own two brothers, Castor and Polydeuces, and thought that they kept aloof in shame for her sin; but the green grass covered their graves, for they had both died in battle, far away in Lacedaemon, their own country.

Then the lambs were sacrificed, and the oaths were taken, and Paris put on his brother's armour, helmet, breastplate, shield, and leg-armour. Lots were drawn to decide whether Paris or Menelaus should throw his spear first, and, as Paris won, he threw his spear, but the point was blunted against the shield of Menelaus. But when Menelaus threw his spear it went clean through the shield of Paris, and through the side of his breastplate, but only grazed his robe. Menelaus drew his sword, and rushed in, and smote at the crest of the helmet of Paris, but his bronze blade broke into four pieces. Menelaus caught Paris by the horsehair crest of his helmet, and dragged him towards the Greeks, but the chin- strap broke, and Menelaus turning round threw the helmet into the ranks of the Greeks. But when Menelaus looked again for Paris, with a spear in his hand, he could see him nowhere! The Greeks believed that the beautiful goddess Aphrodite, whom the Romans called Venus, hid him in a thick cloud of darkness and carried him to his own house, where Helen of the fair hands found him and said to him, "Would that thou hadst perished, conquered by that great warrior who was my lord! Go forth again and challenge him to fight thee face to face. " But Paris had no more desire to fight, and the Goddess threatened Helen, and compelled her to remain with him in Troy, coward as he had proved himself. Yet on other days Paris fought well; it seems that he was afraid of Menelaus because, in his heart, he was ashamed of himself.

Meanwhile Menelaus was seeking for Paris everywhere, and the Trojans, who hated him, would have shown his hiding place. But they knew not where he was, and the Greeks claimed the victory, and thought that, as Paris had the worst of the fight, Helen would be restored to them, and they would all sail home.

TROJAN VICTORIES

The war might now have ended, but an evil and foolish thought came to Pandarus, a prince of Ida, who fought for the Trojans. He chose to shoot an arrow at Menelaus, contrary to the sworn vows of peace, and the arrow pierced the breastplate of Menelaus through the place where the clasped plates meet, and drew his blood. Then Agamemnon, who loved his brother dearly, began to lament, saying that if he died, the army would all go home and Trojans would dance on the grave of Menelaus. "Do not alarm all our army, " said Menelaus, "the arrow has done me little harm; " and so it proved, for the surgeon easily drew the arrow out of the wound.

Then Agamemnon hastened here and there, bidding the Greeks arm and attack the Trojans, who would certainly be defeated, for they had broken the oaths of peace. But with his usual insolence he chose to accuse Ulysses and Diomede of cowardice, though Diomede was as brave as any man, and Ulysses had just prevented the whole army from launching their ships and going home. Ulysses answered him with spirit, but Diomede said nothing at the moment; later he spoke his mind. He leaped from his chariot, and all the chiefs leaped down and advanced in line, the chariots following them, while the spearmen and bowmen followed the chariots. The Trojan army advanced, all shouting in their different languages, but the Greeks came on silently. Then the two front lines clashed, shield against shield, and the noise was like the roaring of many flooded torrents among the hills. When a man fell he who had slain him tried to strip off his armour, and his friends fought over his body to save the dead from this dishonour.

Ulysses fought above a wounded friend, and drove his spear through head and helmet of a Trojan prince, and everywhere men were falling beneath spears and arrows and heavy stones which the warriors threw. Here Menelaus speared the man who built the ships with which Paris had sailed to Greece; and the dust rose like a cloud, and a mist went up from the fighting men, while Diomede stormed across the plain like a river in flood, leaving dead bodies behind him as the river leaves boughs of trees and grass to mark its course. Pandarus wounded Diomede with an arrow, but Diomede slew him, and the Trojans were being driven in flight, when Sarpedon and Hector turned and hurled themselves on the Greeks; and even Diomede shuddered when Hector came on, and charged at Ulysses, who was slaying Trojans as he went, and the battle swayed this way and that, and the arrows fell like rain.

But Hector was sent into the city to bid the women pray to the goddess Athene for help, and he went to the house of Paris, whom Helen was imploring to go and fight like a man, saying: "Would that the winds had wafted me away, and the tides drowned me, shameless that I am, before these things came to pass! "

Then Hector went to see his dear wife, Andromache, whose father had been slain by Achilles early in the siege, and he found her and her nurse carrying her little boy, Hector's son, and like a star upon her bosom lay his beautiful and shining golden head. Now, while Helen urged Paris to go into the fight, Andromache prayed Hector to stay with her in the town, and fight no more lest he should be slain and leave her a widow, and the boy an orphan, with none to protect him. The army she said, should come back within the walls, where they had so long been safe, not fight in the open plain. But Hector answered that he would never shrink from battle, "yet I know this in my heart, the day shall come for holy Troy to be laid low, and Priam and the people of Priam. But this and my own death do not trouble me so much as the thought of you, when you shall be carried as a slave to Greece, to spin at another woman's bidding, and bear water from a Grecian well. May the heaped up earth of my tomb cover me ere I hear thy cries and the tale of thy captivity. "

Then Hector stretched out his hands to his little boy, but the child was afraid when he saw the great glittering helmet of his father and the nodding horsehair crest. So Hector laid his helmet on the ground and dandled the child in his arms, and tried to comfort his wife, and said good-bye for the last time, for he never came back to Troy alive. He went on his way back to the battle, and Paris went with him, in glorious armour, and soon they were slaying the princes of the Greeks.

The battle raged till nightfall, and in the night the Greeks and Trojans burned their dead; and the Greeks made a trench and wall round their camp, which they needed for safety now that the Trojans came from their town and fought in the open plain.

Next day the Trojans were so successful that they did not retreat behind their walls at night, but lit great fires on the plain: a thousand fires, with fifty men taking supper round each of them, and drinking their wine to the music of flutes. But the Greeks were much discouraged, and Agamemnon called the whole army together, and proposed that they should launch their ships in the night and sail away home. Then Diomede stood up, and said: "You called me a coward lately. You are the coward! Sail away if you are afraid to remain here, but all the rest of us will fight till we take Troy town. "

Then all shouted in praise of Diomede, and Nestor advised them to send five hundred young men, under his own son, Thrasymedes, to watch the Trojans, and guard the new wall and the ditch, in case the Trojans attacked them in the darkness. Next Nestor counselled Agamemnon to send Ulysses and Aias to Achilles, and promise to give back Briseis, and rich presents of gold, and beg pardon for his insolence. If Achilles would be friends again with Agamemnon, and fight as he used to fight, the Trojans would soon be driven back into the town.

Agamemnon was very ready to beg pardon, for he feared that the whole army would be defeated, and cut off from their ships, and killed or kept as slaves. So Ulysses and Aias and the old tutor of Achilles, Phoenix, went to Achilles and argued with him, praying him to accept the rich presents, and help the Greeks. But Achilles answered that he did not believe a word that Agamemnon said; Agamemnon had always hated him, and always would hate him. No; he would not cease to be angry, he would sail away next day with all his men, and he advised the rest to come with him. "Why be so fierce? " said tall Aias, who seldom spoke. "Why make so much trouble about one girl? We offer you seven girls, and plenty of other gifts. "

Then Achilles said that he would not sail away next day, but he would not fight till the Trojans tried to burn his own ships, and there he thought that Hector would find work enough to do. This was the most that Achilles would promise, and all the Greeks were silent when Ulysses delivered his message. But Diomede arose and said that, with or without Achilles, fight they must; and all men, heavy at heart, went to sleep in their huts or in the open air at their doors.

Agamemnon was much too anxious to sleep. He saw the glow of the thousand fires of the Trojans in the dark, and heard their merry flutes, and he groaned and pulled out his long hair by handfuls. When he was tired of crying and groaning and tearing his hair, he thought that he would go for advice to old Nestor. He threw a lion skin, the coverlet of his bed, over his shoulder, took his spear, went out and met Menelaus—for he, too, could not sleep—and Menelaus proposed to send a spy among the Trojans, if any man were brave enough to go, for the Trojan camp was all alight with fires, and the adventure was dangerous. Therefore the two wakened Nestor and the other chiefs, who came just as they were, wrapped in the fur coverlets of their beds, without any armour. First they visited the five hundred young men set to watch the wall, and then they crossed the ditch and sat down outside and considered what might be done. "Will nobody go as a spy among the Trojans? " said Nestor; he meant would none of the young men go. Diomede said that he would take the risk if any other man would share it with him, and, if he might choose a companion, he would take Ulysses.

"Come, then, let us be going, " said Ulysses, "for the night is late, and the dawn is near. " As these two chiefs had no armour on, they borrowed shields and leather caps from the young men of the guard, for leather would not shine as bronze helmets shine in the firelight. The cap lent to Ulysses was strengthened outside with rows of boars' tusks. Many of these tusks, shaped for this purpose, have been found, with swords and armour, in a tomb in Mycenae, the town of Agamemnon. This cap which was lent to Ulysses had once been stolen by his grandfather, Autolycus, who was a Master Thief, and he gave it as a present to a friend, and so, through several hands, it had come to young Meriones of Crete, one of the five hundred guards, who now lent it to Ulysses. So the two princes set forth in the dark, so dark it was that though they heard a heron cry, they could not see it as it flew away.

While Ulysses and Diomede stole through the night silently, like two wolves among the bodies of dead men, the Trojan leaders met and considered what they ought to do. They did not know whether the Greeks had set sentinels and outposts, as usual, to give warning if the enemy were approaching; or whether they were too weary to keep a good watch; or whether perhaps they were getting ready their ships to sail homewards in the dawn. So Hector offered a reward to any man who would creep through the night and spy on the Greeks; he said he would give the spy the two best horses in the Greek camp.

Now among the Trojans there was a young man named Dolon, the son of a rich father, and he was the only boy in a family of five sisters. He was ugly, but a very swift runner, and he cared for horses

26

more than for anything else in the world. Dolon arose and said, "If you will swear to give me the horses and chariot of Achilles, son of Peleus, I will steal to the hut of Agamemnon and listen and find out whether the Greeks mean to fight or flee. " Hector swore to give these horses, which were the best in the world, to Dolon, so he took his bow and threw a grey wolf's hide over his shoulders, and ran towards the ships of the Greeks.

Now Ulysses saw Dolon as he came, and said to Diomede, "Let us suffer him to pass us, and then do you keep driving him with your spear towards the ships, and away from Troy. " So Ulysses and Diomede lay down among the dead men who had fallen in the battle, and Dolon ran on past them towards the Greeks. Then they rose and chased him as two greyhounds course a hare, and, when Dolon was near the sentinels, Diomede cried "Stand, or I will slay you with my spear! " and he threw his spear just over Dolon's shoulder. So Dolon stood still, green with fear, and with his teeth chattering. When the two came up, he cried, and said that his father was a rich man, who would pay much gold, and bronze, and iron for his ransom.

Ulysses said, "Take heart, and put death out of your mind, and tell us what you are doing here. " Dolon said that Hector had promised him the horses of Achilles if he would go and spy on the Greeks. "You set your hopes high, " said Ulysses, "for the horses of Achilles are not earthly steeds, but divine; a gift of the Gods, and Achilles alone can drive them. But, tell me, do the Trojans keep good watch, and where is Hector with his horses? " for Ulysses thought that it would be a great adventure to drive away the horses of Hector.

"Hector is with the chiefs, holding council at the tomb of Ilus, " said Dolon; "but no regular guard is set. The people of Troy, indeed, are round their watch fires, for they have to think of the safety of their wives and children; but the allies from far lands keep no watch, for their wives and children are safe at home. " Then he told where all the different peoples who fought for Priam had their stations; but, said he, "if you want to steal horses, the best are those of Rhesus, King of the Thracians, who has only joined us to-night. He and his men are asleep at the furthest end of the line, and his horses are the best and greatest that ever I saw: tall, white as snow, and swift as the wind, and his chariot is adorned with gold and silver, and golden is his armour. Now take me prisoner to the ships, or bind me and leave me here while you go and try whether I have told you truth or lies. "

"No, " said Diomede, "if I spare your life you may come spying again, " and he drew his sword and smote off the head of Dolon. They hid his cap and bow and spear where they could find them easily, and marked the spot, and went through the night to the dark camp of King Rhesus, who had no watch- fire and no guards. Then Diomede silently stabbed each sleeping man to the heart, and Ulysses seized the dead by the feet and threw them aside lest they should frighten the horses, which had never been in battle, and would shy if they were led over the bodies of dead men. Last of all Diomede killed King Rhesus, and Ulysses led forth his horses, beating them with his bow, for he had forgotten to take the whip from the chariot. Then Ulysses and Diomede leaped on the backs of the horses, as they had not time to bring away the chariot, and they galloped to the ships, stopping to pick up the spear, and bow, and cap of Dolon. They rode to the princes, who welcomed them, and all laughed for glee when they saw the white horses and heard that King Rhesus was dead, for they guessed that all his army would now go home to Thrace. This they must have done, for we never hear of them in the battles that followed, so Ulysses and Diomede deprived the Trojans of thousands of men. The other princes went to bed in good spirits, but Ulysses and Diomede took a swim in the sea, and then went into hot baths, and so to breakfast, for rosy- fingered Dawn was coming up the sky.

BATTLE AT THE SHIPS

With dawn Agamemnon awoke, and fear had gone out of his heart. He put on his armour, and arrayed the chiefs on foot in front of their chariots, and behind them came the spearmen, with the bowmen and slingers on the wings of the army. Then a great black cloud spread over the sky, and red was the rain that fell from it. The Trojans gathered on a height in the plain, and Hector, shining in armour, went here and there, in front and rear, like a star that now gleams forth and now is hidden in a cloud.

The armies rushed on each other and hewed each other down, as reapers cut their way through a field of tall corn. Neither side gave ground, though the helmets of the bravest Trojans might be seen deep in the ranks of the Greeks; and the swords of the bravest Greeks rose and fell in the ranks of the Trojans, and all the while the arrows showered like rain. But at noon-day, when the weary woodman rests from cutting trees, and takes his dinner in the quiet hills, the Greeks of the first line made a charge, Agamemnon running in front of them, and he speared two Trojans, and took their breastplates, which he laid in his chariot, and then he speared one brother of Hector and struck another down with his sword, and killed two more who vainly asked to be made prisoners of war. Footmen slew footmen, and chariot men slew chariot men, and they broke into the Trojan line as fire falls on a forest in a windy day, leaping and roaring and racing through the trees. Many an empty chariot did the horses hurry madly through the field, for the charioteers were lying dead, with the greedy vultures hovering above them, flapping their wide wings. Still Agamemnon followed and slew the hindmost Trojans, but the rest fled till they came to the gates, and the oak tree that grew outside the gates, and there they stopped.

But Hector held his hands from fighting, for in the meantime he was making his men face the enemy and form up in line and take breath, and was encouraging them, for they had retreated from the wall of the Greeks across the whole plain, past the hill that was the tomb of Ilus, a king of old, and past the place of the wild fig-tree. Much ado had Hector to rally the Trojans, but he knew that when men do turn again they are hard to beat. So it proved, for when the Trojans had rallied and formed in line, Agamemnon slew a Thracian chief who had come to fight for Troy before King Rhesus came. But the eldest brother of the slain man smote Agamemnon through the arm with his spear, and, though Agamemnon slew him in turn, his wound bled much and he was in great pain, so he leaped into his chariot and was driven back to the ships.

Then Hector gave the word to charge, as a huntsman cries on his hounds against a lion, and he rushed forward at the head of the Trojan line, slaying as he went. Nine chiefs of the Greeks he slew, and fell upon the spearmen and scattered them, as the spray of the waves is scattered by the wandering wind.

Now the ranks of the Greeks were broken, and they would have been driven among their ships and killed without mercy, had not Ulysses and Diomede stood firm in the centre, and slain four Trojan leaders. The Greeks began to come back and face their enemies in line of battle again, though Hector, who had been fighting on the Trojan right, rushed against them. But Diomede took good aim with his spear at the helmet of Hector, and struck it fairly. The spear-point did not go through the helmet, but Hector was stunned and fell; and, when he came to himself, he leaped into his chariot, and his squire drove him against the Pylians and Cretans, under Nestor and Idomeneus, who were on the left wing of the Greek army. Then Diomede fought on till Paris, who stood beside the pillar on the hillock that was the tomb of old King Ilus, sent an arrow clean through his foot. Ulysses went and stood in front of Diomede, who sat down, and Ulysses drew the arrow from his foot, and Diomede stepped into his chariot and was driven back to the ships.

Ulysses was now the only Greek chief that still fought in the centre. The Greeks all fled, and he was alone in the crowd of Trojans, who rushed on him as hounds and hunters press round a wild boar that stands at bay in a wood. "They are cowards that flee from the fight, " said Ulysses to himself; "but I will stand here, one man against a multitude. " He covered the front of his body with his great shield, that hung by a belt round his neck, and he smote four Trojans and wounded a fifth. But the brother of the wounded man drove a spear through the shield and breastplate of Ulysses, and tore clean through his side. Then Ulysses turned on this Trojan, and he fled, and Ulysses sent a spear through his shoulder and out at his breast, and he died. Ulysses dragged from his own side the spear that had wounded him, and called thrice with a great voice to the other Greeks, and Menelaus and Aias rushed to rescue him, for many Trojans were round him, like jackals round a wounded stag that a man has struck with an arrow. But Aias ran and covered the wounded Ulysses with his huge shield till he could climb into the chariot of Menelaus, who drove him back to the ships.

Meanwhile, Hector was slaying the Greeks on the left of their battle, and Paris struck the Greek surgeon, Machaon, with an arrow; and Idomeneus bade Nestor put Machaon in his chariot and drive him to Nestor's hut, where his wound might be tended. Meanwhile, Hector sped to the centre of the line, where Aias was slaying the Trojans; but Eurypylus, a Greek chief, was wounded by an arrow from the bow of Paris, and his friends guarded him with their shields and spears.

Thus the best of the Greeks were wounded and out of the battle, save Aias, and the spearmen were in flight. Meanwhile Achilles was standing by the stern of his ship watching the defeat of the Greeks, but when he saw Machaon being carried past, sorely wounded, in the chariot of Nestor, he bade his friend Patroclus, whom he loved better than all the rest, to go and ask how Machaon did. He was sitting drinking wine with Nestor when Patroclus came, and Nestor told Patroclus how many of the chiefs were wounded, and though Patroclus was in a hurry Nestor began a very long story about his own great deeds of war, done when he was a young man. At last he bade Patroclus tell Achilles that, if he would not fight himself, he should at least send out his men under Patroclus, who should wear the splendid armour of Achilles. Then the Trojans would think that Achilles himself had returned to the battle, and they would be afraid, for none of them dared to meet Achilles hand to hand.

So Patroclus ran off to Achilles; but, on his way, he met the wounded Eurypylus, and he took him to his hut and cut the arrow out of his thigh with a knife, and washed the wound with warm water, and rubbed over it a bitter root to take the pain away. Thus he waited for some time with Eurypylus, but the advice of Nestor was in the end to cause the death of Patroclus. The battle now raged more fiercely, while Agamemnon and Diomede and Ulysses could only limp about leaning on their spears; and again Agamemnon wished to moor the ships near shore, and embark in the night and run away. But Ulysses was very angry with him, and said: "You should lead some other inglorious army, not us, who will fight on till every soul of us perish, rather than flee like cowards! Be silent, lest the soldiers hear you speaking of flight, such words as no man should utter. I wholly scorn your counsel, for the Greeks will lose heart if, in the midst of battle, you bid them launch the ships. "

Agamemnon was ashamed, and, by Diomede's advice, the wounded kings went down to the verge of the war to encourage the others, though they were themselves unable to fight. They rallied the Greeks, and Aias led them and struck Hector full in the breast with a great rock, so that his friends carried him out of the battle to the river side, where they poured water over him, but he lay fainting on the ground, the black blood gushing up from his mouth. While Hector lay there, and all men thought that he would die, Aias and Idomeneus were driving back the Trojans, and it seemed that, even without Achilles and his men, the Greeks were able to hold their own against the Trojans. But the battle was never lost while Hector lived. People in those days believed in "omens: " they thought that the appearance of birds on the right or left hand meant good or bad luck. Once during the battle a Trojan showed Hector an unlucky bird, and wanted him to retreat into the town. But Hector said, "One omen is the best: to fight for our own country. " While Hector lay between death and life the Greeks were winning, for the Trojans had no other great chief to lead them. But Hector awoke from his faint, and leaped to his feet and ran here and there, encouraging the men of Troy. Then the most of the Greeks fled when they saw him; but Aias and Idomeneus, and the rest of the bravest, formed in a square between the Trojans and the ships, and down on them came Hector and Aeneas and Paris, throwing their spears, and slaying on every hand. The Greeks turned and ran, and the Trojans would have stopped to strip the armour from the slain men, but Hector cried: "Haste to the ships and leave the spoils of war. I will slay any man who lags behind! "

On this, all the Trojans drove their chariots down into the ditch that guarded the ships of the Greeks, as when a great wave sweeps at sea over the side of a vessel; and the Greeks were on the ship decks, thrusting with very long spears, used in sea fights, and the Trojans were boarding the ships, and striking with swords and axes. Hector had a lighted torch and tried to set fire to the ship of Aias; but Aias kept him back with the long spear, and slew a Trojan, whose lighted torch fell from his hand. And Aias kept shouting: "Come on, and drive away Hector; it is not to a dance that he is calling his men, but to battle. "

The dead fell in heaps, and the living ran over them to mount the heaps of slain and climb the ships. Hector rushed forward like a sea wave against a great steep rock, but like the rock stood the Greeks; still the Trojans charged past the beaks of the foremost ships, while Aias, thrusting with a spear more than twenty feet long, leaped from deck to deck like a man that drives four horses abreast, and leaps from the back of one to the back of another. Hector seized with his hand the stern of the ship of Protesilaus, the prince whom Paris shot when he leaped ashore on the day when the Greeks first landed; and Hector kept calling: "Bring fire! " and even Aias, in this strange sea fight on land, left the decks and went below, thrusting with his spear through the portholes. Twelve men lay dead who had brought fire against the ship which Aias guarded.

THE SLAYING AND AVENGING OF PATROCLUS

At this moment, when torches were blazing round the ships, and all seemed lost, Patroclus came out of the hut of Eurypylus, whose wound he had been tending, and he saw that the Greeks were in great danger, and ran weeping to Achilles. "Why do you weep, " said Achilles, "like a little girl that runs by her mother's side, and plucks at her gown and looks at her with tears in her eyes, till her mother takes her up in her arms? Is there bad news from home that your father is dead, or mine; or are you sorry that the Greeks are getting what they deserve for their folly? " Then Patroclus told Achilles how Ulysses and many other princes were wounded and could not fight, and begged to be allowed to put on Achilles' armour and lead his men, who were all fresh and unwearied, into the battle, for a charge of two thousand fresh warriors might turn the fortune of the day.

Then Achilles was sorry that he had sworn not to fight himself till Hector brought fire to his own ships. He would lend Patroclus his armour, and his horses, and his men; but Patroclus must only drive the Trojans from the ships, and not pursue them. At this moment Aias was weary, so many spears smote his armour, and he could hardly hold up his great shield, and Hector cut off his spear-head with the sword; the bronze head fell ringing on the ground, and Aias brandished only the pointless shaft. So he shrank back and fire blazed all over his ship; and Achilles saw it, and smote his thigh, and bade Patroclus make haste. Patroclus armed himself in the shining armour of Achilles, which all Trojans feared, and leaped into the chariot where Automedon, the squire, had harnessed Xanthus and Balius, two horses that were the children, men said, of the West Wind, and a led horse was harnessed beside them in the side traces. Meanwhile the two thousand men of Achilles, who were called Myrmidons, had met in armour, five companies of four hundred apiece, under five chiefs of noble names. Forth they came, as eager as a pack of wolves that have eaten a great red deer and run to slake their thirst with the dark water of a well in the hills.

So all in close array, helmet touching helmet and shield touching shield, like a moving wall of shining bronze, the men of Achilles charged, and Patroclus, in the chariot led the way. Down they came at full speed on the flank of the Trojans, who saw the leader, and knew the bright armour and the horses of the terrible Achilles, and thought that he had returned to the war. Then each Trojan looked round to see by what way he could escape, and when men do that in battle they soon run by the way they have chosen. Patroclus rushed to the ship of Protesilaus, and slew the leader of the Trojans there, and drove them out, and quenched the fire; while they of Troy drew back from the ships, and Aias and the other unwounded Greek princes leaped among them, smiting with sword and spear. Well did Hector know that the break in the battle had come again; but even so he stood, and did what he might, while the Trojans were driven back in disorder across the ditch, where the poles of many chariots were broken and the horses fled loose across the plain.

The horses of Achilles cleared the ditch, and Patroclus drove them between the Trojans and the wall of their own town, slaying many men, and, chief of all, Sarpedon, king of the Lycians; and round the body of Sarpedon the Trojans rallied under Hector, and the fight swayed this way and that, and there was such a noise of spears and swords smiting shields and helmets as when many woodcutters fell trees in a glen of the hills. At last the Trojans gave way, and the Greeks stripped the armour from the body of brave Sarpedon; but men say that Sleep and Death, like two winged angels, bore his body away to his own country. Now Patroclus forgot how Achilles had told him not to pursue the Trojans across the plain, but to return when he had driven them from the ships. On he raced, slaying as he went, even till he reached the foot of the wall of Troy. Thrice he tried to climb it, but thrice he fell back.

Hector was in his chariot in the gateway, and he bade his squire lash his horses into the war, and struck at no other man, great or small, but drove straight against Patroclus, who stood and threw a heavy stone at Hector; which missed him, but killed his charioteer. Then Patroclus leaped on the charioteer to strip his armour, but Hector stood over the body, grasping it by the head, while Patroclus dragged at the feet, and spears and arrows flew in clouds around the fallen man. At last, towards sunset, the Greeks drew him out of the war, and Patroclus thrice charged into the thick of the Trojans. But the helmet of Achilles was loosened in the fight, and fell from the head of Patroclus, and he was wounded from behind, and Hector, in front, drove his spear clean through his body. With his last breath Patroclus prophesied: "Death stands near thee, Hector, at the hands of noble Achilles. " But Automedon was driving back the swift horses, carrying to Achilles the news that his dearest friend was slain.

After Ulysses was wounded, early in this great battle, he was not able to fight for several days, and, as the story is about Ulysses, we must tell quite shortly how Achilles returned to the war to take vengeance for Patroclus, and how he slew Hector. When Patroclus fell, Hector seized the armour which the Gods had given to Peleus, and Peleus to his son Achilles, while Achilles had lent it to Patroclus that he might terrify the Trojans. Retiring out of reach of spears, Hector took off his own armour and put on that of Achilles, and Greeks and Trojans fought for the dead body of Patroclus. Then Zeus, the chief of the Gods, looked down and said that Hector should never come home out of the battle to his wife, Andromache. But Hector returned into the fight around the dead Patroclus, and here all the best men fought, and even Automedon, who had been driving the chariot of Patroclus. Now when the Trojans seemed to have the better of the fight, the Greeks sent Antilochus, a son of old Nestor, to tell Achilles that his friend was slain, and Antilochus ran, and Aias and his brother protected the Greeks who were trying to carry the body of Patroclus back to the ships.

Swiftly Antilochus came running to Achilles, saying: "Fallen is Patroclus, and they are fighting round his naked body, for Hector has his armour. " Then Achilles said never a word, but fell on the floor of his hut, and threw black ashes on his yellow hair, till Antilochus seized his hands, fearing that he would cut his own throat with his dagger, for very sorrow. His mother, Thetis, arose from the sea to comfort him, but he said that he desired to die if he could not slay Hector, who had slain his friend. Then Thetis told him that he could not fight without armour, and now he had none; but she would go to the God of armour-making and bring from him such a shield and helmet and breastplate as had never been seen by men.

Meanwhile the fight raged round the dead body of Patroclus, which was defiled with blood and dust, near the ships, and was being dragged this way and that, and torn and wounded. Achilles could not bear this sight, yet his mother had warned him not to enter without armour the battle where stones and arrows and spears were flying like hail; and he was so tall and broad that he could put on the arms of no other man. So he went down to the ditch as he was, unarmed, and as he stood high above it, against the red sunset, fire seemed to flow from his golden hair like the beacon blaze that soars into the dark sky when an island town is attacked at night, and men light beacons that their neighbours may see them and come to their help from other isles. There Achilles stood in a splendour of fire, and he shouted aloud, as clear as a clarion rings when men fall on to attack a besieged city wall. Thrice Achilles shouted mightily, and thrice the horses of the Trojans shuddered for fear and turned back from the onslaught, —and thrice the men of Troy were confounded and shaken with terror. Then the Greeks drew the body of Patroclus out of the dust and the arrows, and laid him on a bier, and Achilles followed, weeping, for he had sent his friend with chariot and horses to the war; but home again he welcomed him never more. Then the sun set and it was night.

Now one of the Trojans wished Hector to retire within the walls of Troy, for certainly Achilles would to-morrow be foremost in the war. But Hector said, "Have ye not had your fill of being shut up behind walls? Let Achilles fight; I will meet him in the open field. " The Trojans cheered, and they camped in the plain, while in the hut of Achilles women washed the dead body of Patroclus, and Achilles swore that he would slay Hector.

In the dawn came Thetis, bearing to Achilles the new splendid armour that the God had made for him. Then Achilles put on that armour, and roused his men; but Ulysses, who knew all the rules of honour, would not let him fight till peace had been made, with a sacrifice and other ceremonies, between him and Agamemnon, and till Agamemnon had given him all the presents which Achilles had before refused. Achilles did not want them; he wanted only to fight, but Ulysses made him obey, and do what was usual. Then the gifts were brought, and Agamemnon stood up, and said that he was sorry for his insolence, and the men took breakfast, but Achilles would neither eat nor drink. He mounted his chariot, but the horse Xanthus bowed his head till his long mane touched the ground, and, being a fairy horse, the child of the West Wind, he spoke (or so men said), and these were his words: "We shall bear thee swiftly and speedily, but thou shalt be slain in fight, and thy dying day is near at hand. " "Well I know it, " said Achilles, "but I will not cease from fighting till I have given the Trojans their fill of war. "

So all that day he chased and slew the Trojans. He drove them into the river, and, though the river came down in a red flood, he crossed, and slew them on the plain. The plain caught fire, the bushes and long dry grass blazed round him, but he fought his way through the fire, and drove the Trojans to their walls. The gates were thrown open, and the Trojans rushed through like frightened fawns, and then they climbed to the battlements, and looked down in safety, while the whole Greek army advanced in line under their shields.

But Hector stood still, alone, in front of the gate, and old Priam, who saw Achilles rushing on, shining like a star in his new armour, called with tears to Hector, "Come within the gate! This man has slain many of my sons, and if he slays thee whom have I to help me in my old age? " His mother also called to Hector, but he stood firm, waiting for Achilles. Now the story says that he was afraid, and ran thrice in full armour round Troy, with Achilles in pursuit. But this cannot be true, for no mortal men could run thrice, in heavy armour, with great shields that clanked against their ankles, round the town of Troy: moreover Hector was the bravest of men, and all the Trojan women were looking down at him from the walls.

We cannot believe that he ran away, and the story goes on to tell that he asked Achilles to make an agreement with him. The conqueror in the fight should give back the body of the fallen to be buried by his friends, but should keep his armour. But Achilles said that he could make no agreement with Hector, and threw his spear, which flew over Hector's shoulder. Then Hector threw his spear, but it could not pierce the shield which the God had made for Achilles. Hector had no other spear, and Achilles had one, so Hector cried, "Let me not die without honour! " and drew his sword, and rushed at Achilles, who sprang to meet him, but before Hector could come within a sword-stroke Achilles had sent his spear clean through the neck of Hector. He fell in the dust and Achilles said, "Dogs and birds shall tear your flesh unburied. " With his dying breath Hector prayed him to take gold from Priam, and give back his body to be burned in Troy. But Achilles said, "Hound! would that I could bring myself to carve and eat thy raw flesh, but dogs shall devour it, even if thy father offered me thy weight in gold. " With his last words Hector prophesied and said, "Remember me in the day when Paris shall slay thee in the Scaean gate. " Then his brave soul went to the land of the Dead, which the Greeks called Hades. To that land Ulysses sailed while he was still a living man, as the story tells later.

Then Achilles did a dreadful deed; he slit the feet of dead Hector from heel to ankle, and thrust thongs through, and bound him by the thongs to his chariot and trailed the body in the dust. All the women of Troy who were on the walls raised a shriek, and Hector's wife, Andromache, heard the sound. She had been in an inner room of her house, weaving a purple web, and embroidering flowers on it, and she was calling her bower maidens to make ready a bath for Hector when he should come back tired from battle. But when she heard the cry from the wall she trembled, and the shuttle with which she was weaving fell from her hands. "Surely I heard the cry of my husband's mother, " she said, and she bade two of her maidens come with her to see why the people lamented.

She ran swiftly, and reached the battlements, and thence she saw her dear husband's body being whirled through the dust towards the ships, behind the chariot of Achilles. Then night came over her eyes and she fainted. But when she returned to herself she cried out that now none would defend her little boy, and other children would push him away from feasts, saying, "Out with you; no father of thine is at our table, " and his father, Hector, would lie naked at the ships, unclad, unburned, unlamented. To be unburned and unburied was thought the greatest of misfortunes, because the dead man unburned could not go into the House of Hades, God of the Dead, but must always wander, alone and comfortless, in the dark borderland between the dead and the living.

THE CRUELTY OF ACHILLES, AND THE RANSOMING OF HECTOR

When Achilles was asleep that night the ghost of Patroclus came, saying, "Why dost thou not burn and bury me? for the other shadows of dead men suffer me not to come near them, and lonely I wander along the dark dwelling of Hades. " Then Achilles awoke, and he sent men to cut down trees, and make a huge pile of fagots and logs. On this they laid Patroclus, covered with white linen, and then they slew many cattle, and Achilles cut the throats of twelve Trojan prisoners of war, meaning to burn them with Patroclus to do him honour. This was a deed of shame, for Achilles was mad with sorrow and anger for the death of his friend. Then they drenched with wine the great pile of wood, which was thirty yards long and broad, and set fire to it, and the fire blazed all through the night and died down in the morning. They put the white bones of Patroclus in a golden casket, and laid it in the hut of Achilles, who said that, when he died, they must burn his body, and mix the ashes with the ashes of his friend, and build over it a chamber of stone, and cover the chamber with a great hill of earth, and set a pillar of stone above it. This is one of the hills on the plain of Troy, but the pillar has fallen from the tomb, long ago.

Then, as the custom was, Achilles held games—chariot races, foot races, boxing, wrestling, and archery—in honour of Patroclus. Ulysses won the prize for the foot race, and for the wrestling, so now his wound must have been healed.

But Achilles still kept trailing Hector's dead body each day round the hill that had been raised for the tomb of Patroclus, till the Gods in heaven were angry, and bade Thetis tell her son that he must give back the dead body to Priam, and take ransom for it, and they sent a messenger to Priam to bid him redeem the body of his son. It was terrible for Priam to have to go and humble himself before Achilles, whose hands had been red with the blood of his sons, but he did not disobey the Gods. He opened his chests, and took out twenty-four beautiful embroidered changes of raiment; and he weighed out ten heavy bars, or talents, of gold, and chose a beautiful golden cup, and he called nine of his sons, Paris, and Helenus, and Deiphobus, and the rest, saying, "Go, ye bad sons, my shame; would that Hector lived and all of you were dead! " for sorrow made him angry; "go, and get ready for me a wain, and lay on it these treasures. " So they

40

harnessed mules to the wain, and placed in it the treasures, and, after praying, Priam drove through the night to the hut of Achilles. In he went, when no man looked for him, and kneeled to Achilles, and kissed his terrible death-dealing hands. "Have pity on me, and fear the Gods, and give me back my dead son, " he said, "and remember thine own father. Have pity on me, who have endured to do what no man born has ever done before, to kiss the hands that slew my sons."

Then Achilles remembered his own father, far away, who now was old and weak: and he wept, and Priam wept with him, and then Achilles raised Priam from his knees and spoke kindly to him, admiring how beautiful he still was in his old age, and Priam himself wondered at the beauty of Achilles. And Achilles thought how Priam had long been rich and happy, like his own father, Peleus, and now old age and weakness and sorrow were laid upon both of them, for Achilles knew that his own day of death was at hand, even at the doors. So Achilles bade the women make ready the body of Hector for burial, and they clothed him in a white mantle that Priam had brought, and laid him in the wain; and supper was made ready, and Priam and Achilles ate and drank together, and the women spread a bed for Priam, who would not stay long, but stole away back to Troy while Achilles was asleep.

All the women came out to meet him, and to lament for Hector. They carried the body into the house of Andromache and laid it on a bed, and the women gathered around, and each in turn sang her song over the great dead warrior. His mother bewailed him, and his wife, and Helen of the fair hands, clad in dark mourning raiment, lifted up her white arms, and said: "Hector, of all my brethren in Troy thou wert the dearest, since Paris brought me hither. Would that ere that day I had died! For this is now the twentieth year since I came, and in all these twenty years never heard I a word from thee that was bitter and unkind; others might upbraid me, thy sisters or thy mother, for thy father was good to me as if he had been my own; but then thou wouldst restrain them that spoke evil by the courtesy of thy heart and thy gentle words. Ah! woe for thee, and woe for me, whom all men shudder at, for there is now none in wide Troyland to be my friend like thee, my brother and my friend! "

So Helen lamented, but now was done all that men might do; a great pile of wood was raised, and Hector was burned, and his ashes were placed in a golden urn, in a dark chamber of stone, within a hollow hill.

HOW ULYSSES STOLE THE LUCK OF TROY

After Hector was buried, the siege went on slowly, as it had done during the first nine years of the war. The Greeks did not know at that time how to besiege a city, as we saw, by way of digging trenches and building towers, and battering the walls with machines that threw heavy stones. The Trojans had lost courage, and dared not go into the open plain, and they were waiting for the coming up of new armies of allies — the Amazons, who were girl warriors from far away, and an Eastern people called the Khita, whose king was Memnon, the son of the Bright Dawn.

Now everyone knew that, in the temple of the Goddess Pallas Athene, in Troy, was a sacred image, which fell from heaven, called the Palladium, and this very ancient image was the Luck of Troy. While it remained safe in the temple people believed that Troy could never be taken, but as it was in a guarded temple in the middle of the town, and was watched by priestesses day and night, it seemed impossible that the Greeks should ever enter the city secretly and steal the Luck away.

As Ulysses was the grandson of Autolycus, the Master Thief, he often wished that the old man was with the Greeks, for if there was a thing to steal Autolycus could steal it. But by this time Autolycus was dead, and so Ulysses could only puzzle over the way to steal the Luck of Troy, and wonder how his grandfather would have set about it. He prayed for help secretly to Hermes, the God of Thieves, when he sacrificed goats to him, and at last he had a plan.

There was a story that Anius, the King of the Isle of Delos, had three daughters, named OEno, Spermo, and Elais, and that OEno could turn water into wine, while Spermo could turn stones into bread, and Elais could change mud into olive oil. Those fairy gifts, people said, were given to the maidens by the Wine God, Dionysus, and by the Goddess of Corn, Demeter. Now corn, and wine, and oil were sorely needed by the Greeks, who were tired of paying much gold and bronze to the Phoenician merchants for their supplies. Ulysses therefore went to Agamemnon one day, and asked leave to take his ship and voyage to Delos, to bring, if he could, the three maidens to the camp, if indeed they could do these miracles. As no fighting was going on, Agamemnon gave Ulysses leave to depart, so he went on board his ship, with a crew of fifty men of Ithaca, and away they sailed, promising to return in a month.

Two or three days after that, a dirty old beggar man began to be seen in the Greek camp. He had crawled in late one evening, dressed in a dirty smock and a very dirty old cloak, full of holes, and stained with smoke. Over everything he wore the skin of a stag, with half the hair worn off, and he carried a staff, and a filthy tattered wallet, to put food in, which swung from his neck by a cord. He came crouching and smiling up to the door of the hut of Diomede, and sat down just within the doorway, where beggars still sit in the East. Diomede saw him, and sent him a loaf and two handfuls of flesh, which the beggar laid on his wallet, between his feet, and he made his supper greedily, gnawing a bone like a dog.

After supper Diomede asked him who he was and whence he came, and he told a long story about how he had been a Cretan pirate, and had been taken prisoner by the Egyptians when he was robbing there, and how he had worked for many years in their stone quarries, where the sun had burned him brown, and had escaped by hiding among the great stones, carried down the Nile in a raft, for building a temple on the seashore. The raft arrived at night, and the beggar said that he stole out from it in the dark and found a Phoenician ship in the harbour, and the Phoenicians took him on board, meaning to sell him somewhere as a slave. But a tempest came on and wrecked the ship off the Isle of Tenedos, which is near Troy, and the beggar alone escaped to the island on a plank of the ship. From Tenedos he had come to Troy in a fisher's boat, hoping to make himself useful in the camp, and earn enough to keep body and soul together till he could find a ship sailing to Crete.

He made his story rather amusing, describing the strange ways of the Egyptians; how they worshipped cats and bulls, and did everything in just the opposite of the Greek way of doing things. So Diomede let him have a rug and blankets to sleep on in the portico of the hut, and next day the old wretch went begging about the camp and talking with the soldiers. Now he was a most impudent and annoying old vagabond, and was always in quarrels. If there was a disagreeable story about the father or grandfather of any of the princes, he knew it and told it, so that he got a blow from the baton of Agamemnon, and Aias gave him a kick, and Idomeneus drubbed him with the butt of his spear for a tale about his grandmother, and everybody hated him and called him a nuisance. He was for ever jeering at Ulysses, who was far away, and telling tales about Autolycus, and at last he stole a gold cup, a very large cup, with two handles, and a dove sitting on each handle, from the hut of Nestor. The old chief was fond of this cup, which he had brought from home, and, when it was found in the beggar's dirty wallet, everybody cried that he must be driven out of the camp and well whipped. So Nestor's son, young Thrasymedes, with other young men, laughing and shouting, pushed and dragged the beggar close up to the Scaean gate of Troy, where Thrasymedes called with a loud voice, "O Trojans, we are sick of this shameless beggar. First we shall whip him well, and if he comes back we shall put out his eyes and cut off his hands and feet, and give him to the dogs to eat. He may go to you, if he likes; if not, he must wander till he dies of hunger. "

The young men of Troy heard this and laughed, and a crowd gathered on the wall to see the beggar punished. So Thrasymedes whipped him with his bowstring till he was tired, and they did not leave off beating the beggar till he ceased howling and fell, all bleeding, and lay still. Then Thrasymedes gave him a parting kick, and went away with his friends. The beggar lay quiet for some time, then he began to stir, and sat up, wiping the tears from his eyes, and shouting curses and bad words after the Greeks, praying that they might be speared in the back, and eaten by dogs.

At last he tried to stand up, but fell down again, and began to crawl on hands and knees towards the Scaean gate. There he sat down, within the two side walls of the gate, where he cried and lamented. Now Helen of the fair hands came down from the gate tower, being sorry to see any man treated so much worse than a beast, and she spoke to the beggar and asked him why he had been used in this cruel way?

At first he only moaned, and rubbed his sore sides, but at last he said that he was an unhappy man, who had been shipwrecked, and was begging his way home, and that the Greeks suspected him of being a spy sent out by the Trojans. But he had been in Lacedaemon, her own country, he said, and could tell her about her father, if she were, as he supposed, the beautiful Helen, and about her brothers, Castor and Polydeuces, and her little daughter, Hermione.

"But perhaps, " he said, "you are no mortal woman, but some goddess who favours the Trojans, and if indeed you are a goddess then I liken you to Aphrodite, for beauty, and stature, and shapeliness. " Then Helen wept; for many a year had passed since she had heard any word of her father, and daughter, and her brothers, who were dead, though she knew it not. So she stretched out her white hand, and raised the beggar, who was kneeling at her feet, and bade him follow her to her own house, within the palace garden of King Priam.

Helen walked forward, with a bower maiden at either side, and the beggar crawling after her. When she had entered her house, Paris was not there, so she ordered the bath to be filled with warm water, and new clothes to be brought, and she herself washed the old beggar and anointed him with oil. This appears very strange to us, for though Saint Elizabeth of Hungary used to wash and clothe beggars, we are surprised that Helen should do so, who was not a saint. But long afterwards she herself told the son of Ulysses, Telemachus, that she had washed his father when he came into Troy disguised as a beggar who had been sorely beaten.

You must have guessed that the beggar was Ulysses, who had not gone to Delos in his ship, but stolen back in a boat, and appeared disguised among the Greeks. He did all this to make sure that nobody could recognise him, and he behaved so as to deserve a whipping that he might not be suspected as a Greek spy by the Trojans, but rather be pitied by them. Certainly he deserved his name of "the much-enduring Ulysses. "

Meanwhile he sat in his bath and Helen washed his feet. But when she had done, and had anointed his wounds with olive oil, and when she had clothed him in a white tunic and a purple mantle, then she opened her lips to cry out with amazement, for she knew Ulysses; but he laid his finger on her lips, saying "Hush! " Then she remembered how great danger he was in, for the Trojans, if they found him, would put him to some cruel death, and she sat down, trembling and weeping, while he watched her.

"Oh thou strange one, " she said, "how enduring is thy heart and how cunning beyond measure! How hast thou borne to be thus beaten and disgraced, and to come within the walls of Troy? Well it is for thee that Paris, my lord, is far from home, having gone to guide Penthesilea, the Queen of the warrior maids whom men call Amazons, who is on her way to help the Trojans. "

Then Ulysses smiled, and Helen saw that she had said a word which she ought not to have spoken, and had revealed the secret hope of the Trojans. Then she wept, and said, "Oh cruel and cunning! You have made me betray the people with whom I live, though woe is me that ever I left my own people, and my husband dear, and my child! And now if you escape alive out of Troy, you will tell the Greeks, and they will lie in ambush by night for the Amazons on the way to Troy and will slay them all. If you and I were not friends long ago, I would tell the Trojans that you are here, and they would give your body to the dogs to eat, and fix your head on the palisade above the wall. Woe is me that ever I was born. "

Ulysses answered, "Lady, as you have said, we two are friends from of old, and your friend I will be till the last, when the Greeks break into Troy, and slay the men, and carry the women captives. If I live till that hour no man shall harm you, but safely and in honour you shall come to your palace in Lacedaemon of the rifted hills. Moreover, I swear to you a great oath, by Zeus above, and by Them that under earth punish the souls of men who swear falsely, that I shall tell no man the thing which you have spoken. "

So when he had sworn and done that oath, Helen was comforted and dried her tears. Then she told him how unhappy she was, and how she had lost her last comfort when Hector died. "Always am I wretched, " she said, "save when sweet sleep falls on me. Now the wife of Thon, King of Egypt, gave me this gift when we were in Egypt, on our way to Troy, namely, a drug that brings sleep even to the most unhappy, and it is pressed from the poppy heads of the garland of the God of Sleep. " Then she showed him strange phials of gold, full of this drug: phials wrought by the Egyptians, and covered with magic spells and shapes of beasts and flowers. "One of these I will give you, " she said, "that even from Troy town you may not go without a gift in memory of the hands of Helen. " So Ulysses took the phial of gold, and was glad in his heart, and Helen set before him meat and wine. When he had eaten and drunk, and his strength had come back to him, he said:

"Now I must dress me again in my old rags, and take my wallet, and my staff, and go forth, and beg through Troy town. For here I must abide for some days as a beggar man, lest if I now escape from your house in the night the Trojans may think that you have told me the secrets of their counsel, which I am carrying to the Greeks, and may be angry with you. " So he clothed himself again as a beggar, and took his staff, and hid the phial of gold with the Egyptian drug in his rags, and in his wallet also he put the new clothes that Helen had given him, and a sword, and he took farewell, saying, "Be of good heart, for the end of your sorrows is at hand. But if you see me among the beggars in the street, or by the well, take no heed of me, only I will salute you as a beggar who has been kindly treated by a Queen. "

So they parted, and Ulysses went out, and when it was day he was with the beggars in the streets, but by night he commonly slept near the fire of a smithy forge, as is the way of beggars. So for some days he begged, saying that he was gathering food to eat while he walked to some town far away that was at peace, where he might find work to do. He was not impudent now, and did not go to rich men's houses or tell evil tales, or laugh, but he was much in the temples, praying to the Gods, and above all in the temple of Pallas Athene. The Trojans thought that he was a pious man for a beggar.

Now there was a custom in these times that men and women who were sick or in distress, should sleep at night on the floors of the temples. They did this hoping that the God would send them a dream to show them how their diseases might be cured, or how they might find what they had lost, or might escape from their distresses.

Ulysses slept in more than one temple, and once in that of Pallas Athene, and the priests and priestesses were kind to him, and gave him food in the morning when the gates of the temple were opened.

In the temple of Pallas Athene, where the Luck of Troy lay always on her altar, the custom was that priestesses kept watch, each for two hours, all through the night, and soldiers kept guard within call. So one night Ulysses slept there, on the floor, with other distressed people, seeking for dreams from the Gods. He lay still all through the night till the turn of the last priestess came to watch. The priestess used to walk up and down with bare feet among the dreaming people, having a torch in her hand, and muttering hymns to the Goddess. Then Ulysses, when her back was turned, slipped the gold phial out of his rags, and let it lie on the polished floor beside him. When the priestess came back again, the light from her torch fell on the glittering phial, and she stooped and picked it up, and looked at it curiously. There came from it a sweet fragrance, and she opened it, and tasted the drug. It seemed to her the sweetest thing that ever she had tasted, and she took more and more, and then closed the phial and laid it down, and went along murmuring her hymn.

But soon a great drowsiness came over her, and she sat down on the step of the altar, and fell sound asleep, and the torch sunk in her hand, and went out, and all was dark. Then Ulysses put the phial in his wallet, and crept very cautiously to the altar, in the dark, and stole the Luck of Troy. It was only a small black mass of what is now called meteoric iron, which sometimes comes down with meteorites from the sky, but it was shaped like a shield, and the people thought it an image of the warlike shielded Goddess, fallen from Heaven. Such sacred shields, made of glass and ivory, are found deep in the earth in the ruined cities of Ulysses' time. Swiftly Ulysses hid the Luck in his rags and left in its place on the altar a copy of the Luck, which he had made of blackened clay. Then he stole back to the place where he had lain, and remained there till dawn appeared, and the sleepers who sought for dreams awoke, and the temple gates were opened, and Ulysses walked out with the rest of them.

He stole down a lane, where as yet no people were stirring, and crept along, leaning on his staff, till he came to the eastern gate, at the back of the city, which the Greeks never attacked, for they had never drawn their army in a circle round the town. There Ulysses explained to the sentinels that he had gathered food enough to last for a long journey to some other town, and opened his bag, which seemed full of bread and broken meat. The soldiers said he was a lucky beggar, and let him out. He walked slowly along the waggon road by which wood was brought into Troy from the forests on Mount Ida, and when he found that nobody was within sight he slipped into the forest, and stole into a dark thicket, hiding beneath the tangled boughs. Here he lay and slept till evening, and then took the new clothes which Helen had given him out of his wallet, and put them on, and threw the belt of the sword over his shoulder, and hid the Luck of Troy in his bosom. He washed himself clean in a mountain brook, and now all who saw him must have known that he was no beggar, but Ulysses of Ithaca, Laertes' son.

So he walked cautiously down the side of the brook which ran between high banks deep in trees, and followed it till it reached the river Xanthus, on the left of the Greek lines. Here he found Greek sentinels set to guard the camp, who cried aloud in joy and surprise, for his ship had not yet returned from Delos, and they could not guess how Ulysses had come back alone across the sea. So two of the sentinels guarded Ulysses to the hut of Agamemnon, where he and Achilles and all the chiefs were sitting at a feast. They all leaped up, but when Ulysses took the Luck of Troy from within his mantle, they cried that this was the bravest deed that had been done in the war, and they sacrificed ten oxen to Zeus.

"So you were the old beggar, " said young Thrasymedes.

"Yes, " said Ulysses, "and when next you beat a beggar, Thrasymedes, do not strike so hard and so long. "

That night all the Greeks were full of hope, for now they had the Luck of Troy, but the Trojans were in despair, and guessed that the beggar was the thief, and that Ulysses had been the beggar. The priestess, Theano, could tell them nothing; they found her, with the extinguished torch drooping in her hand, asleep, as she sat on the step of the altar, and she never woke again.

THE BATTLES WITH THE AMAZONS AND MEMNON—THE DEATH OF ACHILLES

Ulysses thought much and often of Helen, without whose kindness he could not have saved the Greeks by stealing the Luck of Troy. He saw that, though she remained as beautiful as when the princes all sought her hand, she was most unhappy, knowing herself to be the cause of so much misery, and fearing what the future might bring. Ulysses told nobody about the secret which she had let fall, the coming of the Amazons.

The Amazons were a race of warlike maids, who lived far away on the banks of the river Thermodon. They had fought against Troy in former times, and one of the great hill-graves on the plain of Troy covered the ashes of an Amazon, swift-footed Myrine. People believed that they were the daughters of the God of War, and they were reckoned equal in battle to the bravest men. Their young Queen, Penthesilea, had two reasons for coming to fight at Troy: one was her ambition to win renown, and the other her sleepless sorrow for having accidentally killed her sister, Hippolyte, when hunting. The spear which she threw at a stag struck Hippolyte and slew her, and Penthesilea cared no longer for her own life, and desired to fall gloriously in battle. So Penthesilea and her bodyguard of twelve Amazons set forth from the wide streams of Thermodon, and rode into Troy. The story says that they did not drive in chariots, like all the Greek and Trojan chiefs, but rode horses, which must have been the manner of their country.

Penthesilea was the tallest and most beautiful of the Amazons, and shone among her twelve maidens like the moon among the stars, or the bright Dawn among the Hours which follow her chariot wheels. The Trojans rejoiced when they beheld her, for she looked both terrible and beautiful, with a frown on her brow, and fair shining eyes, and a blush on her cheeks. To the Trojans she came like Iris, the Rainbow, after a storm, and they gathered round her cheering, and throwing flowers and kissing her stirrup, as the people of Orleans welcomed Joan of Arc when she came to deliver them. Even Priam was glad, as is a man long blind, when he has been healed, and again looks upon the light of the sun. Priam held a great feast, and gave to Penthesilea many beautiful gifts: cups of gold, and embroideries, and a sword with a hilt of silver, and she vowed that she would slay Achilles. But when Andromache, the wife of Hector, heard her she said within herself, "Ah, unhappy girl, what is this boast of thine! Thou hast not the strength to fight the unconquerable son of Peleus, for if Hector could not slay him, what chance hast thou? But the piled-up earth covers Hector! "

In the morning Penthesilea sprang up from sleep and put on her glorious armour, with spear in hand, and sword at side, and bow and quiver hung behind her back, and her great shield covering her side from neck to stirrup, and mounted her horse, and galloped to the plain. Beside her charged the twelve maidens of her bodyguard, and all the company of Hector's brothers and kinsfolk. These headed the Trojan lines, and they rushed towards the ships of the Greeks.

Then the Greeks asked each other, "Who is this that leads the Trojans as Hector led them, surely some God rides in the van of the charioteers! " Ulysses could have told them who the new leader of the Trojans was, but it seems that he had not the heart to fight against women, for his name is not mentioned in this day's battle. So the two lines clashed, and the plain of Troy ran red with blood, for Penthesilea slew Molios, and Persinoos, and Eilissos, and Antiphates, and Lernos high of heart, and Hippalmos of the loud warcry, and Haemonides, and strong Elasippus, while her maidens Derinoe and Clonie slew each a chief of the Greeks. But Clonie fell beneath the spear of Podarkes, whose hand Penthesilea cut off with the sword, while Idomeneus speared the Amazon Bremousa, and Meriones of Crete slew Evadre, and Diomede killed Alcibie and Derimacheia in close fight with the sword, so the company of the Twelve were thinned, the bodyguard of Penthesilea.

The Trojans and Greeks kept slaying each other, but Penthesilea avenged her maidens, driving the ranks of Greece as a lioness drives the cattle on the hills, for they could not stand before her. Then she shouted, "Dogs! to-day shall you pay for the sorrows of Priam! Where is Diomede, where is Achilles, where is Aias, that, men say, are your bravest? Will none of them stand before my spear? " Then she charged again, at the head of the Household of Priam, brothers and kinsmen of Hector, and where they came the Greeks fell like yellow leaves before the wind of autumn. The white horse that Penthesilea rode, a gift from the wife of the North Wind, flashed like lightning through a dark cloud among the companies of the Greeks, and the chariots that followed the charge of the Amazon rocked as they swept over the bodies of the slain. Then the old Trojans, watching from the walls, cried: "This is no mortal maiden but a

Goddess, and to-day she will burn the ships of the Greeks, and they will all perish in Troyland, and see Greece never more again. "

Now it so was that Aias and Achilles had not heard the din and the cry of war, for both had gone to weep over the great new grave of Patroclus. Penthesilea and the Trojans had driven back the Greeks within their ditch, and they were hiding here and there among the ships, and torches were blazing in men's hands to burn the ships, as in the day of the valour of Hector: when Aias heard the din of battle, and called to Achilles to make speed towards the ships.

So they ran swiftly to their huts, and armed themselves, and Aias fell smiting and slaying upon the Trojans, but Achilles slew five of the bodyguard of Penthesilea. She, beholding her maidens fallen, rode straight against Aias and Achilles, like a dove defying two falcons, and cast her spear, but it fell back blunted from the glorious shield that the God had made for the son of Peleus. Then she threw another spear at Aias, crying, "I am the daughter of the God of War, " but his armour kept out the spear, and he and Achilles laughed aloud. Aias paid no more heed to the Amazon, but rushed against the Trojan men; while Achilles raised the heavy spear that none but he could throw, and drove it down through breastplate and breast of Penthesilea, yet still her hand grasped her sword-hilt. But, ere she could draw her sword, Achilles speared her horse, and horse and rider fell, and died in their fall.

There lay fair Penthesilea in the dust, like a tall poplar tree that the wind has overthrown, and her helmet fell, and the Greeks who gathered round marvelled to see her lie so beautiful in death, like Artemis, the Goddess of the Woods, when she sleeps alone, weary with hunting on the hills. Then the heart of Achilles was pierced with pity and sorrow, thinking how she might have been his wife in his own country, had he spared her, but he was never to see pleasant Phthia, his native land, again. So Achilles stood and wept over Penthesilea dead.

Now the Greeks, in pity and sorrow, held their hands, and did not pursue the Trojans who had fled, nor did they strip the armour from Penthesilea and her twelve maidens, but laid the bodies on biers, and sent them back in peace to Priam. Then the Trojans burned Penthesilea in the midst of her dead maidens, on a great pile of dry wood, and placed their ashes in a golden casket, and buried them all in the great hill-grave of Laomedon, an ancient King of Troy, while the Greeks with lamentation buried them whom the Amazon had slain.

The old men of Troy and the chiefs now held a council, and Priam said that they must not yet despair, for, if they had lost many of their bravest warriors, many of the Greeks had also fallen. Their best plan was to fight only with arrows from the walls and towers, till King Memnon came to their rescue with a great army of Aethiopes. Now Memnon was the son of the bright Dawn, a beautiful Goddess who had loved and married a mortal man, Tithonus. She had asked Zeus, the chief of the Gods, to make her lover immortal, and her prayer was granted. Tithonus could not die, but he began to grow grey, and then white haired, with a long white beard, and very weak, till nothing of him seemed to be left but his voice, always feebly chattering like the grasshoppers on a summer day.

Memnon was the most beautiful of men, except Paris and Achilles, and his home was in a country that borders on the land of sunrising. There he was reared by the lily maidens called Hesperides, till he came to his full strength, and commanded the whole army of the Aethiopes. For their arrival Priam wished to wait, but Polydamas advised that the Trojans should give back Helen to the Greeks, with jewels twice as valuable as those which she had brought from the house of Menelaus. Then Paris was very angry, and said that Polydamas was a coward, for it was little to Paris that Troy should be taken and burned in a month if for a month he could keep Helen of the fair hands.

At length Memnon came, leading a great army of men who had nothing white about them but the teeth, so fiercely the sun burned on them in their own country. The Trojans had all the more hopes of Memnon because, on his long journey from the land of sunrising, and the river Oceanus that girdles the round world, he had been obliged to cross the country of the Solymi. Now the Solymi were the fiercest of men and rose up against Memnon, but he and his army fought them for a whole day, and defeated them, and drove them to the hills. When Memnon came, Priam gave him a great cup of gold, full of wine to the brim, and Memnon drank the wine at one draught. But he did not make great boasts of what he could do, like poor Penthesilea, "for, " said he, "whether I am a good man at arms will be known in battle, where the strength of men is tried. So now let us turn to sleep, for to wake and drink wine all through the night is an ill beginning of war. "

Then Priam praised his wisdom, and all men betook them to bed, but the bright Dawn rose unwillingly next day, to throw light on the battle where her son was to risk his fife. Then Memnon led out the dark clouds of his men into the plain, and the Greeks foreboded evil when they saw so great a new army of fresh and unwearied warriors, but Achilles, leading them in his shining armour, gave them courage. Memnon fell upon the left wing of the Greeks, and on the men of Nestor, and first he slew Ereuthus, and then attacked Nestor's young son, Antilochus, who, now that Patroclus had fallen, was the dearest friend of Achilles. On him Memnon leaped, like a lion on a kid, but Antilochus lifted a huge stone from the plain, a pillar that had been set on the tomb of some great warrior long ago, and the stone smote full on the helmet of Memnon, who reeled beneath the stroke. But Memnon seized his heavy spear, and drove it through shield and corselet of Antilochus, even into his heart, and he fell and died beneath his father's eyes. Then Nestor in great sorrow and anger strode across the body of Antilochus and called to his other son, Thrasymedes, "Come and drive afar this man that has slain thy brother, for if fear be in thy heart thou art no son of mine, nor of the race of Periclymenus, who stood up in battle even against the strong man Heracles! "

But Memnon was too strong for Thrasymedes, and drove him off, while old Nestor himself charged sword in hand, though Memnon bade him begone, for he was not minded to strike so aged a man, and Nestor drew back, for he was weak with age. Then Memnon and his army charged the Greeks, slaying and stripping the dead. But Nestor had mounted his chariot and driven to Achilles, weeping, and imploring him to come swiftly and save the body of Antilochus, and he sped to meet Memnon, who lifted a great stone, the landmark of a field, and drove it against the shield of the son of Peleus. But Achilles was not shaken by the blow; he ran forward, and wounded Memnon over the rim of his shield. Yet wounded as he was Memnon fought on and struck his spear through the arm of Achilles, for the Greeks fought with no sleeves of bronze to protect their arms.

Then Achilles drew his great sword, and flew on Memnon, and with sword- strokes they lashed at each other on shield and helmet, and the long horsehair crests of the helmets were shorn off, and flew down the wind, and their shields rang terribly beneath the sword strokes. They thrust at each others' throats between shield and visor of the helmet, they smote at knee, and thrust at breast, and the armour rang about their bodies, and the dust from beneath their feet rose up in a cloud around them, like mist round the falls of a great river in flood. So they fought, neither of them yielding a step, till Achilles made so rapid a thrust that Memnon could not parry it, and the bronze sword passed clean through his body beneath the breast-bone, and he fell, and his armour clashed as he fell.

Then Achilles, wounded as he was and weak from loss of blood, did not stay to strip the golden armour of Memnon, but shouted his warcry, and pressed on, for he hoped to enter the gate of Troy with the fleeing Trojans, and all the Greeks followed after him. So they pursued, slaying as they went, and the Scaean gate was choked with the crowd of men, pursuing and pursued. In that hour would the Greeks have entered Troy, and burned the city, and taken the women captive, but Paris stood on the tower above the gate, and in his mind was anger for the death of his brother Hector. He tried the string of his bow, and found it frayed, for all day he had showered his arrows on the Greeks; so he chose a new bowstring, and fitted it, and strung the bow, and chose an arrow from his quiver, and aimed at the ankle of Achilles, where it was bare beneath the greave, or leg-guard of metal, that the God had fashioned for him. Through the ankle flew the arrow, and Achilles wheeled round, weak as he was, and stumbled, and fell, and the armour that the God had wrought was defiled with dust and blood.

Then Achilles rose again, and cried: "What coward has smitten me with a secret arrow from afar? Let him stand forth and meet me with sword and spear! " So speaking he seized the shaft with his strong hands and tore it out of the wound, and much blood gushed, and darkness came over his eyes. Yet he staggered forward, striking blindly, and smote Orythaon, a dear friend of Hector, through the helmet, and others he smote, but now his force failed him, and he leaned on his spear, and cried his warcry, and said, "Cowards of Troy, ye shall not all escape my spear, dying as I am. " But as he spoke he fell, and all his armour rang around him, yet the Trojans stood apart and watched; and as hunters watch a dying lion not daring to go nigh him, so the Trojans stood in fear till Achilles drew his latest breath. Then from the wall the Trojan women raised a great cry of joy over him who had slain the noble Hector: and thus was fulfilled the prophecy of Hector, that Achilles should fall in the Scaean gateway, by the hand of Paris.

Then the best of the Trojans rushed forth from the gate to seize the body of Achilles, and his glorious armour, but the Greeks were as eager to carry the body to the ships that it might have due burial. Round the dead Achilles men fought long and sore, and both sides were mixed, Greeks and Trojans, so that men dared not shoot arrows from the walls of Troy lest they should kill their own friends. Paris, and Aeneas, and Glaucus, who had been the friend of Sarpedon, led the Trojans, and Aias and Ulysses led the Greeks, for we are not told that Agamemnon was fighting in this great battle of the war. Now as angry wild bees flock round a man who is taking their honeycombs, so the Trojans gathered round Aias, striving to stab him, but he set his great shield in front, and smote and slew all that came within reach of his spear. Ulysses, too, struck down many, and though a spear was thrown and pierced his leg near the knee he stood firm, protecting the body of Achilles. At last Ulysses caught the body of Achilles by the hands, and heaved it upon his back, and so limped towards the ships, but Aias and the men of Aias followed, turning round if ever the Trojans ventured to come near, and charging into the midst of them. Thus very slowly they bore the dead Achilles across the plain, through the bodies of the fallen and the blood, till they met Nestor in his chariot and placed Achilles therein, and swiftly Nestor drove to the ships.

There the women, weeping, washed Achilles' comely body, and laid him on a bier with a great white mantle over him, and all the women lamented and sang dirges, and the first was Briseis, who loved Achilles better than her own country, and her father, and her brothers whom he had slain in war. The Greek princes, too, stood round the body, weeping and cutting off their long locks of yellow hair, a token of grief and an offering to the dead.

Men say that forth from the sea came Thetis of the silver feet, the mother of Achilles, with her ladies, the deathless maidens of the waters. They rose up from their glassy chambers below the sea, moving on, many and beautiful, like the waves on a summer day, and their sweet song echoed along the shores, and fear came upon the Greeks. Then they would have fled, but Nestor cried: "Hold, flee not, young lords of the Achaeans! Lo, she that comes from the sea is his mother, with the deathless maidens of the waters, to look on the face of her dead son. " Then the sea nymphs stood around the dead Achilles and clothed him in the garments of the Gods, fragrant raiment, and all the Nine Muses, one to the other replying with sweet voices, began their lament.

Next the Greeks made a great pile of dry wood, and laid Achilles on it, and set fire to it, till the flames had consumed his body except the white ashes. These they placed in a great golden cup and mingled with them the ashes of Patroclus, and above all they built a tomb like a hill, high on a headland above the sea, that men for all time may see it as they go sailing by, and may remember Achilles. Next they held in his honour foot races and chariot races, and other games, and Thetis gave splendid prizes. Last of all, when the games were ended, Thetis placed before the chiefs the glorious armour that the God had made for her son on the night after the slaying of Patroclus by Hector. "Let these arms be the prize of the best of the Greeks, " she said, "and of him that saved the body of Achilles out of the hands of the Trojans. "

Then stood up on one side Aias and on the other Ulysses, for these two had rescued the body, and neither thought himself a worse warrior than the other. Both were the bravest of the brave, and if Aias was the taller and stronger, and upheld the fight at the ships on the day of the valour of Hector; Ulysses had alone withstood the Trojans, and refused to retreat even when wounded, and his courage and cunning had won for the Greeks the Luck of Troy. Therefore old Nestor arose and said: "This is a luckless day, when the best of the Greeks are rivals for such a prize. He who is not the winner will be heavy at heart, and will not stand firm by us in battle, as of old, and hence will come great loss to the Greeks. Who can be a just judge in this question, for some men will love Aias better, and some will prefer Ulysses, and thus will arise disputes among ourselves. Lo! have we not here among us many Trojan prisoners, waiting till their friends pay their ransom in cattle and gold and bronze and iron? These hate all the Greeks alike, and will favour neither Aias nor Ulysses. Let *them* be the judges, and decide who is the best of the Greeks, and the man who has done most harm to the Trojans. "

Agamemnon said that Nestor had spoken wisely. The Trojans were then made to sit as judges in the midst of the Assembly, and Aias and Ulysses spoke, and told the stories of their own great deeds, of which we have heard already, but Aias spoke roughly and discourteously, calling Ulysses a coward and a weakling. "Perhaps the Trojans know, " said Ulysses quietly, "whether they think that I deserve what Aias has said about me, that I am a coward; and perhaps Aias may remember that he did not find me so weak when we wrestled for a prize at the funeral of Patroclus. "

Then the Trojans all with one voice said that Ulysses was the best man among the Greeks, and the most feared by them, both for his courage and his skill in stratagems of war. On this, the blood of Aias flew into his face, and he stood silent and unmoving, and could not speak a word, till his friends came round him and led him away to his hut, and there he sat down and would not eat or drink, and the night fell.

Long he sat, musing in his mind, and then rose and put on all his armour, and seized a sword that Hector had given him one day when they two fought in a gentle passage of arms, and took courteous farewell of each other, and Aias had given Hector a broad sword-belt, wrought with gold. This sword, Hector's gift, Aias took, and went towards the hut of Ulysses, meaning to carve him limb from limb, for madness had come upon him in his great grief. Rushing through the night to slay Ulysses he fell upon the flock of sheep that the Greeks kept for their meat. And up and down among them he went, smiting blindly till the dawn came, and, lo! his senses returned to him, and he saw that he had not smitten Ulysses, but stood in a pool of blood among the sheep that he had slain. He could not endure the disgrace of his madness, and he fixed the sword, Hector's gift, with its hilt firmly in the ground, and went back a little way, and ran and fell upon the sword, which pierced his heart, and so died the great Aias, choosing death before a dishonoured life.

ULYSSES SAILS TO SEEK THE SON OF ACHILLES. — THE VALOUR OF EURYPYLUS

When the Greeks found Aias lying dead, slain by his own hand, they made great lament, and above all the brother of Aias, and his wife Tecmessa bewailed him, and the shores of the sea rang with their sorrow. But of all no man was more grieved than Ulysses, and he stood up and said: "Would that the sons of the Trojans had never awarded to me the arms of Achilles, for far rather would I have given them to Aias than that this loss should have befallen the whole army of the Greeks. Let no man blame me, or be angry with me, for I have not sought for wealth, to enrich myself, but for honour only, and to win a name that will be remembered among men in times to come. " Then they made a great fire of wood, and burned the body of Aias, lamenting him as they had sorrowed for Achilles.

Now it seemed that though the Greeks had won the Luck of Troy and had defeated the Amazons and the army of Memnon, they were no nearer taking Troy than ever. They had slain Hector, indeed, and many other Trojans, but they had lost the great Achilles, and Aias, and Patroclus, and Antilochus, with the princes whom Penthesilea and Memnon slew, and the bands of the dead chiefs were weary of fighting, and eager to go home. The chiefs met in council, and Menelaus arose and said that his heart was wasted with sorrow for the death of so many brave men who had sailed to Troy for his sake. "Would that death had come upon me before I gathered this host, " he said, "but come, let the rest of us launch our swift ships, and return each to our own country. "

He spoke thus to try the Greeks, and see of what courage they were, for his desire was still to burn Troy town and to slay Paris with his own hand. Then up rose Diomede, and swore that never would the Greeks turn cowards. No! he bade them sharpen their swords, and make ready for battle. The prophet Calchas, too, arose and reminded the Greeks how he had always foretold that they would take Troy in the tenth year of the siege, and how the tenth year had come, and victory was almost in their hands. Next Ulysses stood up and said that, though Achilles was dead, and there was no prince to lead his men, yet a son had been born to Achilles, while he was in the isle of Scyros, and that son he would bring to fill his father's place.

"Surely he will come, and for a token I will carry to him those unhappy arms of the great Achilles. Unworthy am I to wear them, and they bring back to my mind our sorrow for Aias. But his son will wear them, in the front of the spearmen of Greece and in the thickest ranks of Troy shall the helmet of Achilles shine, as it was wont to do, for always he fought among the foremost. " Thus Ulysses spoke, and he and Diomede, with fifty oarsmen, went on board a swift ship, and sitting all in order on the benches they smote the grey sea into foam, and Ulysses held the helm and steered them towards the isle of Scyros.

Now the Trojans had rest from war for a while, and Priam, with a heavy heart, bade men take his chief treasure, the great golden vine, with leaves and clusters of gold, and carry it to the mother of Eurypylus, the king of the people who dwell where the wide marshlands of the river Cayster clang with the cries of the cranes and herons and wild swans. For the mother of Eurypylus had sworn that never would she let her son go to the war unless Priam sent her the vine of gold, a gift of the gods to an ancient King of Troy.

With a heavy heart, then, Priam sent the golden vine, but Eurypylus was glad when he saw it, and bade all his men arm, and harness the horses to the chariots, and glad were the Trojans when the long line of the new army wound along the road and into the town. Then Paris welcomed Eurypylus who was his nephew, son of his sister Astyoche, a daughter of Priam; but the grandfather of Eurypylus was the famous Heracles, the strongest man who ever lived on earth. So Paris brought Eurypylus to his house, where Helen sat working at her embroideries with her four bower maidens, and Eurypylus marvelled when he saw her, she was so beautiful. But the Khita, the people of Eurypylus, feasted in the open air among the Trojans, by the light of great fires burning, and to the music of pipes and flutes. The Greeks saw the fires, and heard the merry music, and they watched all night lest the Trojans should attack the ships before the dawn. But in the dawn Eurypylus rose from sleep and put on his armour, and hung from his neck by the belt the great shield on which were fashioned, in gold of many colours and in silver, the Twelve Adventures of Heracles, his grandfather; strange deeds that he did, fighting with monsters and giants and with the Hound of Hades, who guards the dwellings of the dead. Then Eurypylus led on his whole army, and with the brothers of Hector he charged against the Greeks, who were led by Agamemnon.

In that battle Eurypylus first smote Nireus, who was the most beautiful of the Greeks now that Achilles had fallen. There lay Nireus, like an apple tree, all covered with blossoms red and white, that the wind has overthrown in a rich man's orchard. Then Eurypylus would have stripped off his armour, but Machaon rushed in, Machaon who had been wounded and taken to the tent of Nestor, on the day of the Valour of Hector, when he brought fire against the ships. Machaon drove his spear through the left shoulder of Eurypylus, but Eurypylus struck at his shoulder with his sword, and the blood flowed; nevertheless, Machaon stooped, and grasped a great stone, and sent it against the helmet of Eurypylus. He was shaken, but he did not fall, he drove his spear through breastplate and breast of Machaon, who fell and died. With his last breath he said, "Thou, too, shalt fall, " but Eurypylus made answer, "So let it be! Men cannot live for ever, and such is the fortune of war. "

Thus the battle rang, and shone, and shifted, till few of the Greeks kept steadfast, except those with Menelaus and Agamemnon, for Diomede and Ulysses were far away upon the sea, bringing from Scyros the son of Achilles. But Teucer slew Polydamas, who had warned Hector to come within the walls of Troy; and Menelaus wounded Deiphobus, the bravest of the sons of Priam who were still in arms, for many had fallen; and Agamemnon slew certain spearmen of the Trojans. Round Eurypylus fought Paris, and Aeneas, who wounded Teucer with a great stone, breaking in his helmet, but he drove back in his chariot to the ships. Menelaus and Agamemnon stood alone and fought in the crowd of Trojans, like two wild boars that a circle of hunters surrounds with spears, so fiercely they stood at bay. There they would both have fallen, but Idomeneus, and Meriones of Crete, and Thrasymedes, Nestor's son, ran to their rescue, and fiercer grew the fighting. Eurypylus desired to slay Agamemnon and Menelaus, and end the war, but, as the spears of the Scots encompassed King James at Flodden Field till he ran forward, and fell within a lance's length of the English general, so the men of Crete and Pylos guarded the two princes with their spears.

There Paris was wounded in the thigh with a spear, and he retreated a little way, and showered his arrows among the Greeks; and Idomeneus lifted and hurled a great stone at Eurypylus which struck his spear out of his hand, and he went back to find it, and Menelaus and Agamemnon had a breathing space in the battle. But soon Eurypylus returned, crying on his men, and they drove back foot by foot the ring of spears round Agamemnon, and Aeneas and Paris slew men of Crete and of Mycenae till the Greeks were pushed to the ditch round the camp; and then great stones and spears and arrows rained down on the Trojans and the people of Eurypylus from the battlements and towers of the Grecian wall. Now night fell, and Eurypylus knew that he could not win the wall in the dark, so he withdrew his men, and they built great fires, and camped upon the plain.

The case of the Greeks was now like that of the Trojans after the death of Hector. They buried Machaon and the other chiefs who had fallen, and they remained within their ditch and their wall, for they dared not come out into the open plain. They knew not whether Ulysses and Diomede had come safely to Scyros, or whether their ship had been wrecked or driven into unknown seas. So they sent a herald to Eurypylus, asking for a truce, that they might gather their dead and burn them, and the Trojans and Khita also buried their dead.

Meanwhile the swift ship of Ulysses had swept through the sea to Scyros, and to the palace of King Lycomedes. There they found Neoptolemus, the son of Achilles, in the court before the doors. He was as tall as his father, and very like him in face and shape, and he was practising the throwing of the spear at a mark. Right glad were Ulysses and Diomede to behold him, and Ulysses told Neoptolemus who they were, and why they came, and implored him to take pity on the Greeks and help them.

"My friend is Diomede, Prince of Argos, " said Ulysses, "and I am Ulysses of Ithaca. Come with us, and we Greeks will give you countless gifts, and I myself will present you with the armour of your father, such as it is not lawful for any other mortal man to wear, seeing that it is golden, and wrought by the hands of a God. Moreover, when we have taken Troy, and gone home, Menelaus will give you his daughter, the beautiful Hermione, to be your wife, with gold in great plenty. "

Then Neoptolemus answered: "It is enough that the Greeks need my sword. To-morrow we shall sail for Troy. " He led them into the palace to dine, and there they found his mother, beautiful Deidamia, in mourning raiment, and she wept when she heard that they had come to take her son away. But Neoptolemus comforted her, promising to return safely with the spoils of Troy, "or, even if I fall, " he said, "it will be after doing deeds worthy of my father's name. " So next day they sailed, leaving Deidamia mournful, like a swallow whose nest a serpent has found, and has killed her young ones; even so she wailed, and went up and down in the house. But the ship ran swiftly on her way, cleaving the dark waves till Ulysses showed Neoptolemus the far off snowy crest of Mount Ida; and Tenedos, the island near Troy; and they passed the plain where the tomb of Achilles stands, but Ulysses did not tell the son that it was his father's tomb.

Now all this time the Greeks, shut up within their wall and fighting from their towers, were looking back across the sea, eager to spy the ship of Ulysses, like men wrecked on a desert island, who keep watch every day for a sail afar off, hoping that the seamen will touch at their isle and have pity upon them, and carry them home, so the Greeks kept watch for the ship bearing Neoptolemus.

Diomede, too, had been watching the shore, and when they came in sight of the ships of the Greeks, he saw that they were being besieged by the Trojans, and that all the Greek army was penned up within the wall, and was fighting from the towers. Then he cried aloud to Ulysses and Neoptolemus, "Make haste, friends, let us arm before we land, for some great evil has fallen upon the Greeks. The Trojans are attacking our wall, and soon they will burn our ships, and for us there will be no return. "

Then all the men on the ship of Ulysses armed themselves, and Neoptolemus, in the splendid armour of his father, was the first to leap ashore. The Greeks could not come from the wall to welcome him, for they were fighting hard and hand-to-hand with Eurypylus and his men. But they glanced back over their shoulders and it seemed to them that they saw Achilles himself, spear and sword in hand, rushing to help them. They raised a great battle-cry, and, when Neoptolemus reached the battlements, he and Ulysses, and Diomede leaped down to the plain, the Greeks following them, and they all charged at once on the men of Eurypylus, with levelled spears, and drove them from the wall.

Then the Trojans trembled, for they knew the shields of Diomede and Ulysses, and they thought that the tall chief in the armour of Achilles was Achilles himself, come back from the land of the dead to take vengeance for Antilochus. The Trojans fled, and gathered round Eurypylus, as in a thunderstorm little children, afraid of the lightning and the noise, run and cluster round their father, and hide their faces on his knees.

But Neoptolemus was spearing the Trojans, as a man who carries at night a beacon of fire in his boat on the sea spears the fishes that flock around, drawn by the blaze of the flame. Cruelly he avenged his father's death on many a Trojan, and the men whom Achilles had led followed Achilles' son, slaying to right and left, and smiting the Trojans, as they ran, between the shoulders with the spear. Thus they fought and followed while daylight lasted, but when night fell, they led Neoptolemus to his father's hut, where the women washed him in the bath, and then he was taken to feast with Agamemnon and Menelaus and the princes. They all welcomed him, and gave him glorious gifts, swords with silver hilts, and cups of gold and silver, and they were glad, for they had driven the Trojans from their wall, and hoped that to-morrow they would slay Eurypylus, and take Troy town.

But their hope was not to be fulfilled, for though next day Eurypylus met Neoptolemus in the battle, and was slain by him, when the Greeks chased the Trojans into their city so great a storm of lightning and thunder and rain fell upon them that they retreated again to their camp. They believed that Zeus, the chief of the Gods, was angry with them, and the days went by, and Troy still stood unconquered.

THE SLAYING OF PARIS

When the Greeks were disheartened, as they often were, they consulted Calchas the prophet. He usually found that they must do something, or send for somebody, and in doing so they diverted their minds from their many misfortunes. Now, as the Trojans were fighting more bravely than before, under Deiphobus, a brother of Hector, the Greeks went to Calchas for advice, and he told them that they must send Ulysses and Diomede to bring Philoctetes the bowman from the isle of Lemnos. This was an unhappy deserted island, in which the married women, some years before, had murdered all their husbands, out of jealousy, in a single night. The Greeks had landed in Lemnos, on their way to Troy, and there Philoctetes had shot an arrow at a great water dragon which lived in a well within a cave in the lonely hills. But when he entered the cave the dragon bit him, and, though he killed it at last, its poisonous teeth wounded his foot. The wound never healed, but dripped with venom, and Philoctetes, in terrible pain, kept all the camp awake at night by his cries.

The Greeks were sorry for him, but he was not a pleasant companion, shrieking as he did, and exuding poison wherever he came. So they left him on the lonely island, and did not know whether he was alive or dead. Calchas ought to have told the Greeks not to desert Philoctetes at the time, if he was so important that Troy, as the prophet now said, could not be taken without him. But now, as he must give some advice, Calchas said that Philoctetes must be brought back, so Ulysses and Diomede went to bring him. They sailed to Lemnos, a melancholy place they found it, with no smoke rising from the ruinous houses along the shore. As they were landing they learned that Philoctetes was not dead, for his dismal old cries of pain, *otototoi, ai, ai; pheu, pheu; otototoi*, came echoing from a cave on the beach. To this cave the princes went, and found a terrible-looking man, with long, dirty, dry hair and beard; he was worn to a skeleton, with hollow eyes, and lay moaning in a mass of the feathers of sea birds. His great bow and his arrows lay ready to his hand: with these he used to shoot the sea birds, which were all that he had to eat, and their feathers littered all the floor of his cave, and they were none the better for the poison that dripped from his wounded foot.

When this horrible creature saw Ulysses and Diomede coming near, he seized his bow and fitted a poisonous arrow to the string, for he hated the Greeks, because they had left him in the desert isle. But the princes held up their hands in sign of peace, and cried out that they had come to do him kindness, so he laid down his bow, and they came in and sat on the rocks, and promised that his wound should be healed, for the Greeks were very much ashamed of having deserted him. It was difficult to resist Ulysses when he wished to persuade any one, and at last Philoctetes consented to sail with them to Troy. The oarsmen carried him down to the ship on a litter, and there his dreadful wound was washed with warm water, and oil was poured into it, and it was bound up with soft linen, so that his pain grew less fierce, and they gave him a good supper and wine enough, which he had not tasted for many years.

Next morning they sailed, and had a fair west wind, so that they soon landed among the Greeks and carried Philoctetes on shore. Here Podaleirius, the brother of Machaon, being a physician, did all that could be done to heal the wound, and the pain left Philoctetes. He was taken to the hut of Agamemnon, who welcomed him, and said that the Greeks repented of their cruelty. They gave him seven female slaves to take care of him, and twenty swift horses, and twelve great vessels of bronze, and told him that he was always to live with the greatest chiefs and feed at their table. So he was bathed, and his hair was cut and combed and anointed with oil, and soon he was eager and ready to fight, and to use his great bow and poisoned arrows on the Trojans. The use of poisoned arrow-tips was thought unfair, but Philoctetes had no scruples.

Now in the next battle Paris was shooting down the Greeks with his arrows, when Philoctetes saw him, and cried: "Dog, you are proud of your archery and of the arrow that slew the great Achilles. But, behold, I am a better bowman than you, by far, and the bow in my hands was borne by the strong man Heracles!" So he cried and drew the bowstring to his breast and the poisoned arrowhead to the bow, and the bowstring rang, and the arrow flew, and did but graze the hand of Paris. Then the bitter pain of the poison came upon him, and the Trojans carried him into their city, where the physicians tended him all night. But he never slept, and lay tossing in agony till dawn, when he said: "There is but one hope. Take me to OEnone, the nymph of Mount Ida!"

Then his friends laid Paris on a litter, and bore him up the steep path to Mount Ida. Often had he climbed it swiftly, when he was young, and went to see the nymph who loved him; but for many a day he had not trod the path where he was now carried in great pain and fear, for the poison turned his blood to fire. Little hope he had, for he knew how cruelly he had deserted OEnone, and he saw that all the birds which were disturbed in the wood flew away to the left hand, an omen of evil.

At last the bearers reached the cave where the nymph OEnone lived, and they smelled the sweet fragrance of the cedar fire that burned on the floor of the cave, and they heard the nymph singing a melancholy song. Then Paris called to her in the voice which she had once loved to hear, and she grew very pale, and rose up, saying to herself, "The day has come for which I have prayed. He is sore hurt, and has come to bid me heal his wound. " So she came and stood in the doorway of the dark cave, white against the darkness, and the bearers laid Paris on the litter at the feet of OEnone, and he stretched forth his hands to touch her knees, as was the manner of suppliants. But she drew back and gathered her robe about her, that he might not touch it with his hands.

Then he said: "Lady, despise me not, and hate me not, for my pain is more than I can bear. Truly it was by no will of mine that I left you lonely here, for the Fates that no man may escape led me to Helen. Would that I had died in your arms before I saw her face! But now I beseech you in the name of the Gods, and for the memory of our love, that you will have pity on me and heal my hurt, and not refuse your grace and let me die here at your feet. "

Then OEnone answered scornfully: "Why have you come here to me? Surely for years you have not come this way, where the path was once worn with your feet. But long ago you left me lonely and lamenting, for the love of Helen of the fair hands. Surely she is much more beautiful than the love of your youth, and far more able to help you, for men say that she can never know old age and death. Go home to Helen and let her take away your pain. "

Thus OEnone spoke, and went within the cave, where she threw herself down among the ashes of the hearth and sobbed for anger and sorrow. In a little while she rose and went to the door of the cave, thinking that Paris had not been borne away back to Troy, but she found him not; for his bearers had carried him by another path, till he died beneath the boughs of the oak trees. Then his bearers carried him swiftly down to Troy, where his mother bewailed him, and Helen sang over him as she had sung over Hector, remembering many things, and fearing to think of what her own end might be. But the Trojans hastily built a great pile of dry wood, and thereon laid the body of Paris and set fire to it, and the flame went up through the darkness, for now night had fallen.

But OEnone was roaming in the dark woods, crying and calling after Paris, like a lioness whose cubs the hunters have carried away. The moon rose to give her light, and the flame of the funeral fire shone against the sky, and then OEnone knew that Paris had died— beautiful Paris—and that the Trojans were burning his body on the plain at the foot of Mount Ida. Then she cried that now Paris was all her own, and that Helen had no more hold on him: "And though when he was living he left me, in death we shall not be divided," she said, and she sped down the hill, and through the thickets where the wood nymphs were wailing for Paris, and she reached the plain, and, covering her head with her veil like a bride, she rushed through the throng of Trojans. She leaped upon the burning pile of wood, she clasped the body of Paris in her arms, and the flame of fire consumed the bridegroom and the bride, and their ashes mingled. No man could divide them any more, and the ashes were placed in a golden cup, within a chamber of stone, and the earth was mounded above them. On that grave the wood nymphs planted two rose trees, and their branches met and plaited together.

This was the end of Paris and OEnone.

HOW ULYSSES INVENTED THE DEVICE OF THE HORSE OF TREE

After Paris died, Helen was not given back to Menelaus. We are often told that only fear of the anger of Paris had prevented the Trojans from surrendering Helen and making peace. Now Paris could not terrify them, yet for all that the men of the town would not part with Helen, whether because she was so beautiful, or because they thought it dishonourable to yield her to the Greeks, who might put her to a cruel death. So Helen was taken by Deiphobus, the brother of Paris, to live in his own house, and Deiphobus was at this time the best warrior and the chief captain of the men of Troy.

Meanwhile, the Greeks made an assault against the Trojan walls and fought long and hardily; but, being safe behind the battlements, and shooting through loopholes, the Trojans drove them back with loss of many of their men. It was in vain that Philoctetes shot his poisoned arrows, they fell back from the stone walls, or stuck in the palisades of wood above the walls, and the Greeks who tried to climb over were speared, or crushed with heavy stones. When night fell, they retreated to the ships and held a council, and, as usual, they asked the advice of the prophet Calchas. It was the business of Calchas to go about looking at birds, and taking omens from what he saw them doing, a way of prophesying which the Romans also used, and some savages do the same to this day. Calchas said that yesterday he had seen a hawk pursuing a dove, which hid herself in a hole in a rocky cliff. For a long while the hawk tried to find the hole, and follow the dove into it, but he could not reach her. So he flew away for a short distance and hid himself; then the dove fluttered out into the sunlight, and the hawk swooped on her and killed her.

The Greeks, said Calchas, ought to learn a lesson from the hawk, and take Troy by cunning, as by force they could do nothing. Then Ulysses stood up and described a trick which it is not easy to understand. The Greeks, he said, ought to make an enormous hollow horse of wood, and place the bravest men in the horse. Then all the rest of the Greeks should embark in their ships and sail to the Isle of Tenedos, and lie hidden behind the island. The Trojans would then come out of the city, like the dove out of her hole in the rock, and would wander about the Greek camp, and wonder why the great horse of tree had been made, and why it had been left behind. Lest they should set fire to the horse, when they would soon have found out the warriors hidden in it, a cunning Greek, whom the Trojans did not know by sight, should be left in the camp or near it. He would tell the Trojans that the Greeks had given up all hope and gone home, and he was to say that they feared the Goddess Pallas was angry with them, because they had stolen her image that fell from heaven, and was called the Luck of Troy. To soothe Pallas and prevent her from sending great storms against the ships, the Trojans (so the man was to say) had built this wooden horse as an offering to the Goddess. The Trojans, believing this story, would drag the horse into Troy, and, in the night, the princes would come out, set fire to the city, and open the gates to the army, which would return from Tenedos as soon as darkness came on.

The prophet was much pleased with the plan of Ulysses, and, as two birds happened to fly away on the right hand, he declared that the stratagem would certainly be lucky. Neoptolemus, on the other hand, voted for taking Troy, without any trick, by sheer hard fighting. Ulysses replied that if Achilles could not do that, it could not be done at all, and that Epeius, a famous carpenter, had better set about making the horse at once.

Next day half the army, with axes in their hands, were sent to cut down trees on Mount Ida, and thousands of planks were cut from the trees by Epeius and his workmen, and in three days he had finished the horse. Ulysses then asked the best of the Greeks to come forward and go inside the machine; while one, whom the Greeks did not know by sight, should volunteer to stay behind in the camp and deceive the Trojans. Then a young man called Sinon stood up and said that he would risk himself and take the chance that the Trojans might disbelieve him, and burn him alive. Certainly, none of the Greeks did anything more courageous, yet Sinon had not been considered brave.

Had he fought in the front ranks, the Trojans would have known him; but there were many brave fighters who would not have dared to do what Sinon undertook.

Then old Nestor was the first that volunteered to go into the horse; but Neoptolemus said that, brave as he was, he was too old, and that he must depart with the army to Tenedos. Neoptolemus himself would go into the horse, for he would rather die than turn his back on Troy. So Neoptolemus armed himself and climbed into the horse,

70

as did Menelaus, Ulysses, Diomede, Thrasymedes (Nestor's son), Idomeneus, Philoctetes, Meriones, and all the best men except Agamemnon, while Epeius himself entered last of all. Agamemnon was not allowed by the other Greeks to share their adventure, as he was to command the army when they returned from Tenedos. They meanwhile launched their ships and sailed away.

But first Menelaus had led Ulysses apart, and told him that if they took Troy (and now they must either take it or die at the hands of the Trojans), he would owe to Ulysses the glory. When they came back to Greece, he wished to give Ulysses one of his own cities, that they might always be near each other. Ulysses smiled and shook his head; he could not leave Ithaca, his own rough island kingdom. "But if we both live through the night that is coming, " he said, "I may ask you for one gift, and giving it will make you none the poorer. " Then Menelaus swore by the splendour of Zeus that Ulysses could ask him for no gift that he would not gladly give; so they embraced, and both armed themselves and went up into the horse. With them were all the chiefs except Nestor, whom they would not allow to come, and Agamemnon, who, as chief general, had to command the army. They swathed themselves and their arms in soft silks, that they might not ring and clash, when the Trojans, if they were so foolish, dragged the horse up into their town, and there they sat in the dark waiting. Meanwhile, the army burned their huts and launched their ships, and with oars and sails made their way to the back of the isle of Tenedos.

THE END OF TROY AND THE SAVING OF HELEN

From the walls the Trojans saw the black smoke go up thick into the sky, and the whole fleet of the Greeks sailing out to sea. Never were men so glad, and they armed themselves for fear of an ambush, and went cautiously, sending forth scouts in front of them, down to the seashore. Here they found the huts burned down and the camp deserted, and some of the scouts also caught Sinon, who had hid himself in a place where he was likely to be found. They rushed on him with fierce cries, and bound his hands with a rope, and kicked and dragged him along to the place where Priam and the princes were wondering at the great horse of tree. Sinon looked round upon them, while some were saying that he ought to be tortured with fire to make him tell all the truth about the horse. The chiefs in the horse must have trembled for fear lest torture should wring the truth out of Sinon, for then the Trojans would simply burn the machine and them within it.

But Sinon said: "Miserable man that I am, whom the Greeks hate and the Trojans are eager to slay! " When the Trojans heard that the Greeks hated him, they were curious, and asked who he was, and how he came to be there. "I will tell you all, oh King! " he answered Priam. "I was a friend and squire of an unhappy chief, Palamedes, whom the wicked Ulysses hated and slew secretly one day, when he found him alone, fishing in the sea. I was angry, and in my folly I did not hide my anger, and my words came to the ears of Ulysses. From that hour he sought occasion to slay me. Then Calchas—" here he stopped, saying: "But why tell a long tale? If you hate all Greeks alike, then slay me; this is what Agamemnon and Ulysses desire; Menelaus would thank you for my head. "

The Trojans were now more curious than before. They bade him go on, and he said that the Greeks had consulted an Oracle, which advised them to sacrifice one of their army to appease the anger of the Gods and gain a fair wind homewards. "But who was to be sacrificed? They asked Calchas, who for fifteen days refused to speak. At last, being bribed by Ulysses, he pointed to me, Sinon, and said that I must be the victim. I was bound and kept in prison, while they built their great horse as a present for Pallas Athene the Goddess. They made it so large that you Trojans might never be able to drag it into your city; while, if you destroyed it, the Goddess might turn her anger against you. And now they have gone home to bring back the image that fell from heaven, which they had sent to Greece, and to restore it to the Temple of Pallas Athene, when they have taken your town, for the Goddess is angry with them for that theft of Ulysses. "

The Trojans were foolish enough to believe the story of Sinon, and they pitied him and unbound his hands. Then they tied ropes to the wooden horse, and laid rollers in front of it, like men launching a ship, and they all took turns to drag the horse up to the Scaean gate. Children and women put their hands to the ropes and hauled, and with shouts and dances, and hymns they toiled, till about nightfall the horse stood in the courtyard of the inmost castle.

Then all the people of Troy began to dance, and drink, and sing. Such sentinels as were set at the gates got as drunk as all the rest, who danced about the city till after midnight, and then they went to their homes and slept heavily.

Meanwhile the Greek ships were returning from behind Tenedos as fast as the oarsmen could row them.

One Trojan did not drink or sleep; this was Deiphobus, at whose house Helen was now living. He bade her come with them, for he knew that she was able to speak in the very voice of all men and women whom she had ever seen, and he armed a few of his friends and went with them to the citadel. Then he stood beside the horse, holding Helen's hand, and whispered to her that she must call each of the chiefs in the voice of his wife. She was obliged to obey, and she called Menelaus in her own voice, and Diomede in the voice of his wife, and Ulysses in the very voice of Penelope. Then Menelaus and Diomede were eager to answer, but Ulysses grasped their hands and whispered the word "Echo! " Then they remembered that this was a name of Helen, because she could speak in all voices, and they were silent; but Anticlus was still eager to answer, till Ulysses held his strong hand over his mouth. There was only silence, and Deiphobus led Helen back to his house. When they had gone away Epeius opened the side of the horse, and all the chiefs let themselves down softly to the ground. Some rushed to the gate, to open it, and they killed the sleeping sentinels and let in the Greeks. Others sped with torches to burn the houses of the Trojan princes, and terrible was the slaughter of men, unarmed and half awake, and loud were the cries of the women. But Ulysses had slipped away at the first, none knew where. Neoptolemus ran to the palace of Priam, who was sitting at the altar in his courtyard, praying vainly to the Gods, for Neoptolemus slew the old man cruelly, and his white hair was dabbled in his blood. All through the city was fighting and slaying; but Menelaus went to the house of Deiphobus, knowing that Helen was there.

In the doorway he found Deiphobus lying dead in all his armour, a spear standing in his breast. There were footprints marked in blood, leading through the portico and into the hall. There Menelaus went, and found Ulysses leaning, wounded, against one of the central pillars of the great chamber, the firelight shining on his armour.

"Why hast thou slain Deiphobus and robbed me of my revenge? " said Menelaus. "You swore to give me a gift, " said Ulysses, "and will you keep your oath? " "Ask what you will, " said Menelaus; "it is yours and my oath cannot be broken. " "I ask the life of Helen of the fair hands, " said Ulysses "this is my own life-price that I pay back to her, for she saved my life when I took the Luck of Troy, and I swore that hers should be saved. "

Then Helen stole, glimmering in white robes, from a recess in the dark hall, and fell at the feet of Menelaus; her golden hair lay in the dust of the hearth, and her hands moved to touch his knees. His drawn sword fell from the hands of Menelaus, and pity and love came into his heart, and he raised her from the dust and her white arms were round his neck, and they both wept. That night Menelaus fought no more, but they tended the wound of Ulysses, for the sword of Deiphobus had bitten through his helmet.

When dawn came Troy lay in ashes, and the women were being driven with spear shafts to the ships, and the men were left unburied, a prey to dogs and all manner of birds. Thus the grey city fell, that had lorded it for many centuries. All the gold and silver and rich embroideries, and ivory and amber, the horses and chariots, were divided among the army; all but a treasure of silver and gold, hidden in a chest within a hollow of the wall, and this treasure was found, not very many years ago, by men digging deep on the hill where Troy once stood. The women, too, were given to the princes, and Neoptolemus took Andromache to his home in Argos, to draw water from the well and to be the slave of a master, and Agamemnon carried beautiful Cassandra, the daughter of Priam, to his palace in Mycenae, where they were both slain in one night. Only Helen was led with honour to the ship of Menelaus.

Tales of Troy: Ulysses the Sacker of Cities

The story of all that happened to Ulysses on his way home from Troy is told in another book, "Tales of the Greek Seas. "

Printed in the United States
108889LV00002B/287/A

9 781406 526486